TROUBLE AT MRS PORTWINE'S

To Frances

John Wood was born in Kent and now lives in Wiltshire with his wife and daughter. He served with the RAF; worked as a forester in Canada and England; manufactured bird-tables; was landlord at 'The Red Lion' in Rode near Bath — and now writes full time.

Of his first book *In a Secret Place* (Wolfhound Press, 1986) *Consumer Choice* wrote: "This sensitive, imaginative and beautifully written book remains with the reader long after the book has been closed."

She had a sensation: a feeling that she was taller than she was.

TROUBLE AT
MRS PORTWINE'S

John Wood

Illustrated by
Jan Nesbitt

WOLFHOUND PRESS

Published 1988 in Great Britain
First published in Ireland, 1987
WOLFHOUND PRESS
68 Mountjoy Square, Dublin 1.

This book is fiction. All characters, incidents and names have no
connection with any persons living or dead. Any apparent
resemblance is purely coincidental.

British Library Cataloguing in Publication Data

Wood, John, *1942–*
  Trouble at Mrs Portwine's
  I. Title
  823'.914 [J]   PZ7

  ISBN 0-86327-147-2 hb

This book is published with the assistance of
The Arts Council (An Comhairle Ealaíon),
Dublin, Ireland.

Cover
Cover
Ty
Pri

CONTENTS

Illustrations

They carried the wood, mossy and sometimes wet, in armfuls.

1

The Gift

The Farrants lived in a two-roomed shed which was never meant to be a home in the first place. Mr Farrants often lit a fire under a tank of creosote by the side of this shed. And he had built a tin-roofed lean-to in order to protect the creosote from the rain.

He also cleaned the field ditches. In return for this work, the owner of the land, Mr Fitz-Maurice, allowed the father and his children to live free of charge in the shed and Mr Farrants was also given the right to cut beansticks and peasticks in the woods.

On the other side of the shed was another lean-to, enclosed by rickety walls. This was the kitchen. Here, Georgie, the girl, cooked on the stove. The smoke from that was sometimes bad enough! And if the wind was blowing in the wrong direction the fumes from the creosote would also come into their shed-home. If the children were there, instead of cursing the smell (which privately he did) Mr Farrants would say, "Come on Georgie! Now Ferdie my son, breathe!" as the wood smoke and the smell of the hot creosote filled the room.

Going to sleep, once, listening to the wind rattling the roof, Georgie said, "Ferdie, d'you think we'll move from here? Because if we did . . ."

"It's alright," he said.

"I know it is. I think so too most of the time. But all the same!"

It was because of the state of their home that the children spent much of their time in the woods, picking primroses and violets, or berries, according to the season. Their fingers became brown with the breaking of the stalks and twigs. Sometimes they helped Mr Farrants carry bundles of beansticks out of the wood. Nearly every day they collected branches for the creosote fire or the kitchen stove. They carried the wood, mossy and sometimes wet, in armfuls, so that it touched their bodies.

In spring and summer it was easier to cook outside because the stove smoked so badly. Georgie used a pot which hung from a chain attached to three iron legs. Of course she could stand clear of the smoke, but sometimes she stood in it, not minding, in order to feel the warmth of the flames.

The winter winds and the summer air took from the children's bodies their own smells and gave to them the smells of fields and distant chimney pots, although it would have been extremely difficult to have had it measured. Certainly the creosote fumes had an effect, and the carrying of hazel sticks which after rain were slippery like river fish and had the same smell. No doubt it was also due to the moss on the firewood, which city people never got to touch in their lives, and the wood smoke, and lastly wisps of smoke when the fat caught as Georgie fried sausages for Mr Farrants, the blue fat-smoke going as it did into her long black hair. It was all of these things and not one in particular which gave the Farrants children a smell which was not the smell of ordinary people.

At the village school they sat on a special bench, alone, because of it.

The schoolmistress, who was a kind lady, in spite of being annoyed by the smell, had once said, when half the pupils were away with colds, "The Farrants children never have colds."

Georgie had said, "Please miss, it's because we breathe in." There was laughter. "I mean, miss," she added, flushing, "our dad says the smell of creosote is good for the chest and colds, which is why we breathe in when he says, miss."

"That will do!" the mistress had said sharply as the laughter continued. She was always considerate to Georgie and Ferdie, as far as she was able, without appearing to favour them. She knew of the conditions at their home.

Yet Mr Fitz-Maurice did not seem to think too kindly of them, nor to relish their presence, in spite of the fact that it was he who was largely responsible for their poverty.

As for his nephew, Gordon, he appeared to be even more

disdainful of them than was his uncle.

*   *   *

The first time Georgie met the boy was when he had simply walked into the kitchen. She had been warming gravy on the stove, the surface of the gravy wrinkling like elephant skin, and had gone to the room where the family sat in the evenings, to put on a pullover. On returning to the kitchen, there he was, looking at the gravy pot!

"Do you know who I am?" he asked, not looking at her.

"No I don't," she replied.

"I am Gordon Buckingham."

She paused, then said slowly, "I don't care much if that is so."

"Mr Fitz-Maurice's nephew."

"I don't see that makes any difference," Georgie said, "we still live here."

"It would be rude if it was a house. Anybody can walk into a shed."

"It's our home," she said, going red. She looked steadily at him, noting the way he held his head because of the starched collar. Why, she thought indignantly, he's only a little bigger than Ferdie. She said, "You heard me!"

Gordon shrugged. His face was a pasty white. He had smooth black hair and black eyes and looked important. "It's no bother to me," he said, as he went. "But my uncle owns it all the same."

As Georgie stirred the gravy she thought of the difference between her and people like Gordon.

Of course the visit also made an impression on the nephew. Pots and pots of blackberry jam and thirty, maybe more, huge horse-mushrooms which Georgie had threaded on a string across the kitchen. He had never seen anything like it! He told others of the visit to the shed, including the tenants who had moved into the newly thatched cottage on his uncle's estate.

Having been asked in for a glass of ginger beer, Gordon decided, feeling rather pleased, that Lady and General Sir Charles Whyke de Bonneville were just like other people he knew: attending to him and even urging him to have another biscuit.

The General had fallen asleep in his chair. Thin white hair neatly brushed, he was dreaming of Afghans, not sitting down over buns and tea with them but chasing them over rough ground where the rocks were too hot to touch.

Lady Eunice talked easily, making him feel at home.

Gordon said, looking at the freshly painted walls thoughtfully, perhaps not sensing that Lady Eunice might find the news disagreeable: "I have just come from the Farrants people's home. Now they live in a hut by the woods. They are sort of gypsies."

"How interesting," she said.

The General twitched in his sleep.

"They used to live here in this cottage before it was done up," Gordon said.

When next day Georgie called with her basket of primroses, Lady Eunice did not at first realise who she was.

"Primroses, miss?" She stared beyond Lady Eunice, who said, "No thank you, child."

Ignoring her, Georgie looked at the freshly painted walls. It was all so different!

"Of course then I realised who it was!" Lady Eunice later declared.

"I will see that it does not happen again. I will speak to them," Mr Fitz-Maurice assured her.

"You are so kind!"

"They are not gypsies exactly. I would not have gypsies on my land."

"And of course, if they had a bath."

"I have known people like that put coal in their baths. Or potatoes," he said.

But the truth was that Georgie and Ferdie cleaned themselves in the kitchen, heating the washing water in the blackened pot outside, so that as often as not the water reeked of smoke. They never went into town to sell their odds and ends without washing, and would stand at the bus stop a mile down the road by Mrs Portwine's, their skin feeling tight and soapy.

*   *   *

Chopped kindling wood sold well even in the spring and early summer, because many of the people who bought it were old and spent whole afternoons in the warmth by their black stoves with their kettles and cats. On the good days, Ferdie's trouser pocket would feel heavy with pennies and silver.

They would sit down in the street to count the money. Often they would go back to the shed without buying anything, but always they would walk by the shops, looking into them. The streets seemed to twist and turn in every direction. Quiet stretches with parked cars, some road lamps flickering and smelling of paraffin. They liked the cakeshops and the teashops, where they could peer open-mouthed through the windows at the well-dressed people. Sometimes a lady would come out, touching her companion's arm with a gloved hand, saying something like: "Oh my dear, I felt so stupid!" or "You should have heard what he said!" or "Never in my life!" Then the ladies would be gone, never seeing or sensing the nearness of Georgie. For a moment she felt she could reach out and touch and be with people like that.

Here she was with Ferdie, selling flowers and kindling so that they could buy things for their home, and there was so much rushing by! So much life and elegance. Rows and rows of buns and cakes and boxes of diamonds and watches. It was like a river, this life which she could not enter.

Then one day she had seen a silver picture frame.

"Ferdie, that frame is big enough for the picture of our mum. We wouldn't have to cut it down."

Hardly bothering, the lady in the shop said, "It's silver. Quite beyond you. Quite."

"That's very good isn't it," Georgie interrupted. "It's partly for my dad's birthday, but it also must be something for our home. There, I'll give you half!" Before the lady had time to protest, she added: "And I'll come back with the other half in a few days."

"Very well, I'll put it away for you. I will put your name on it."

"It's Farrants."

The children did not like walking through the woods late in the day, partly because it meant that they had not sold enough

even to pay for the bus fare back, but also because it was at
times, late in the day, such a strange gathering; an ill lit
congregation of trees and animals. It seemed to have even
halted a town in its tracks.

Although that day they had sold kindling and flowers and
had been able to return home by bus, Georgie was not
content. Ferdie sensed her feelings, curling his bony little
body in one of the chairs by the fire. His brown eyes were
fixed unblinking, as the logs settled down, sending up
plumes of sparks. Mr Farrants had fallen asleep in the other
chair.

"Ferdie, come on! There's tea to get for Dad."

"What about us?"

"And for us too. But Dad wants his sassages now instead of
at breakfast."

"I want jam. That's all I want."

"Well then, get it," Georgie said.

After tea Mr Farrants lit his pipe and several candles with
the same match. In the corner of the room was his bed. "I'll
have an early night my dears," he said, "so off you go to your
room."

Georgie said, "Dad, we've all sorts of seed for planting.
Runner beans, carrot seed. We've hens."

"So we have."

"All free you might say. But sassages!" she said, wanting to
point out that the family's money was being wasted on them.

Mr Farrants replied, "Add a little flavour. You do them to a
turn."

Going to sleep, Georgie thought of their stocks of chicken
and food. Seven hens, one cockerel. She had added to the
number of dried mushrooms. All manner of root vegetables,
and now some damson jam to add to her pots, given to her by
a kind lady in the town.

The candles had burned low.

"Ferdie, are you awake?"

"What's the matter?"

"Well, I wish we weren't spending all that money on
sassages, when we've so much other food besides."

"I knew something was bothering you," Ferdie said.

"And as it's Dad's birthday soon we'll have to tell him he'll get 'is present later. We just haven't got the money."

Mr Farrants opened the door. "Do you want another candle?"

"No, it's alright," said Ferdie.

"And stop talking, else you'll take hours to get off ag'in. And Georgie . . . "

"Dad?"

"There's enough for breakfast. But call in at Mrs Portwine's in the morning and buy some sassages. I'll leave money on the table before I go off to the woods."

A moment later Georgie whispered, "See what I mean? It's a pity his mind is set so hard against stews."

In the cottage days there had been plenty of them. During the cooking the passages had smelled of them, the rooms upstairs had reeked pleasantly of them. They were made from root vegetables, beans, a little rabbit meat, with dumplings and onions. Mr Farrants had loved stews.

But ever since they had lived in the shed there had been no stews, in spite of the fact that they cost so little to make. Once when Georgie had offered to cook one, Mr Farrants' brown eyes had become bright and squirrel-like. He had banged the tobacco ash out of his cherrywood pipe so hard that he broke the stem, saying that not on any account did he want stew.

As Georgie was going to sleep it felt as if her bed was floating, that she herself was floating, having a vision. She could see the cottage again. The yellow roses and leather-bound books; a silver dish! Lady Eunice saying: "What is it child?" It did not exist any more in the way that she remembered.

But there was little space in her life for regrets about how things used to be; certainly not with Mr Farrants' birthday so near.

*   *   *

"I'm short of two shillings, miss." Georgie was standing under the glittering crystal lights, her black hair gleaming, made neat with a little soapy water. Her face and high cheek bones looking whiter than usual: turnip coloured, an old-animal-tooth-locked-in-a-piece-of-bone-in-the-woods colour. A minute must have ticked by, which if the circumstances are particular, can of course be a long time.

The lady opened her purse and placed two shillings in the till. "Now off you go!" she said as gruffly as she could.

Ferdie was outside with the basket. "It's not just a birthday present is it?" he said, "it's to put on the mantelpiece, for all of us, isn't it?"

Georgie ignored this. "We've still got a few primroses left. We must sell them, Ferdie."

But they could not.

His mouth set in a grim line as he felt Georgie's anxiety. He said gruffly: "Primroses. Nice bunch." People were almost backing away because of his manner.

"Oh Ferdie, Ferdie!" said Georgie. Then: "Lady, please lady!"

Ferdie said, "If we don't go now, we'll miss the bus."

Georgie nodded. "And if we don't get on the bus we'll be late at Mrs Portwine's, and we've still got to buy the sassages for Dad."

"So come on then!"

But still Georgie lingered. And they missed the bus!

Georgie gripped the silver frame tightly against her chest and shivered. Ferdie was talking, but she did not listen, saying only, "Alright Ferdie."

"We'd better start walking," he repeated.

Georgie said to herself, again and again, "Why did I do it? Why? What do I do now?"

She had spent the sausage money on the frame.

"Georgie, we'll never get Mrs Portwine to answer the door. She never does after five." He did not know about the money.

They came out of the woods near Mrs Portwine's.

"It won't do us no good, it's after five," said Georgie.

"Well, at least we can try!"

"I'll go round the back, you hold the basket."

Out of Ferdie's sight, she stood in the shadows, watching some gnats circling, and thinking about what to say if Mrs Portwine saw her.

Lying to Ferdie a few minutes later, she said, "No one answered," adding, "I'll tell 'im."

"Tell 'im what?"

"Oh that we got the sassages, in case he wants the money."

Ferdie now knew she was lying in some way, and he had begun to listen closely, ready to support her as he always did when she did not tell the truth. "We've already got two left over from yesterday and 'e won't know."

And later they all stood, Mr Farrants and his children, in the candle-lit shed, with the curtains drawn to. Then Georgie brought the cake in and he ran a finger through his moustache saying: "Ah! My children, well I never!" The loose sheet of roof iron scraped in the wind, and the candle by the picture flickered. "You could not have thought of a better present."

Georgie undid the paper hats. She felt stifled. Ferdie was breathing hard, interested, saying: "Which one have you got Dad?"

Mr Farrants said, almost to himself, "I only wish . . . . " He put on a chocolate-coloured hat with gold edges.

Then Georgie drew the curtains back and the evening bird-songs flooded in. Already she was planning what to do about the sausages. Her eyes were unblinking as she stared out of the window. In ways like this so like her mother!

"Come on Ferdie," said Mr Farrants later, "we'll get some eggs."

He bent down into the laying boxes, feeling for them, saying, "Hello my lovely! Now they'll go nicely with me sassages, won't they?"

2

My Children Don't Steal!

Mrs Portwine's sausages were no ordinary sausages. Mr Portwine used strong skin so that they had to be pricked with a fork, the meat turning brown and crisp where it had burst out. The sausages would twist and pop and become bigger for a moment, collapsing again, releasing juices and fats and herby smells. It was, some said, the choice of herbs that made her sausages so extraordinary. No one knew exactly what she put in them. Even Mr Portwine did not know.

He just stuffed the mixture into the skin with a machine which, being old and in need of replacement, without warning occasionally produced exceedingly small and misshapen sausages. These were given away with good orders and, as Mrs Portwine said, the kind thought pleased customers no end.

It was the fame of her sausages that brought people to Mrs Portwine's roadside café. Not just the short sausages, but the normal ones, "on the string", as she called them, or in the pan. The lorry drivers, and carters going to and from the town, gathered in her rooms, to take away the sausages, or to eat them at one of the small tables together with a pot of tea and a plateful of bread and butter.

The café was set back off the road, so that lorries of all shapes and sizes could stop there. Often there were one or two carts as well, the waiting horses with heads deep down in hessian eating bags fitted around their necks. Each of the café rooms was joined to the other, with no doors in between. Each had a small coal fire which Mrs Portwine occasionally lit when it was cool, regardless of the time of year.

She liked to come from the kitchen, adjusting her dress, checking her hair, then to stop at the tables, asking about the health of the people she knew, or about their children, or their work. It was all very respectful and homely. There was a little coal smoke in the air from one fire in particular.

Sometimes a lorry driver might bang his hand on the table and guffaw with laughter, or a voice would be raised in anger. Then she would leave the counter and come near to their table, adjusting the salt and pepper pots, or she might just pop her head out of the kitchen door; she would look at them and it would become settled again. Or going to the table, "Are the sausages alright?" she might say.

She was slow moving, short, heavily built, with small hands, the fat dimpling on her fingers. She had a way of thrusting her mouth forward, her eyes fixing on the men, as she enquired about their health, the sausages, forcing them, like children, to be well-mannered.

At five o'clock sharp, summer and winter, she would draw the curtains and within minutes the customers would leave. "Goodbye, thank you for calling," she would say, even if they still had sausages on the plate. As the last one left she would call out to her husband, "All gone, Portwine. Lock the door!" After that if anyone knocked at the door they would be ignored. Even if it was only five minutes after five, and all the customer wanted was sausages on a string, as they were called.

On the night of Mr Farrants' birthday there was bright moonlight long after the Portwines had closed the curtains, although not with their usual care. Now a strip of dazzling moonlight showed between them, making the empty chairs and tables gleam.

The night was so moonlit that a person could have bounded down the road without fear of bumping into anything. Or horses galloped with silvered nostrils. Hedge twigs were lined with moonlight. Once or twice cows broke away from their cud-eating and ran across the fields, tails high. Even the mice were covered in downy light; and yet, in dark places in the woods, away from the coughing of the cows, it was as dark as where you might expect dead kings to rest.

A farmer out late on some mysterious journey had not bothered to light his lanterns. The wheels whisked along the road. He was erect, long necked: a strange light-and-dark figure gaping at the white hedges and fields.

Georgie stood at the bedroom window, glancing back at Ferdie. The moonlight shone on his bed. His mouth was relaxed and she thought his lashes looked like a girl's at that moment. She touched him, but he did not stir. Then she covered him with another blanket.

She put candles and matches in her dress pocket. Looking for them in the kitchen cupboard she had mistakenly touched and fingered the two pots of strawberry jam. The sudden cold glass on her fingers had been like a warning, like advice. Her mother had made the jam when they were in the cottage. She had made it and labelled it the week before she had died.

As Georgie made her way to Mrs Portwine's she looked at the dark mansion on the hill, and occasionally shivered. For a moment she thought low lights were showing, which would have been puzzling at that hour of the night, but it was only the moonlight on the panes, silvery like a moth's wing: soft and strange.

Standing by Mrs Portwine's back door, she had a sensation: a feeling that she was taller than she was. She felt unreal, strangely bold. She imagined a star in deep space; a ship against a steady wind; a mouse, still in the night with eyes like jewels from a robber's bag.

The small top window by the back door was still open. It looked just large enough for Georgie. Then, not thinking for one minute that it would open, she idly tried the door. It squealed and groaned! She knew that if she shut it, the noise would start again, so she opened it wider and went in.

On her return Georgie put the stolen sausages in the kitchen.

At first she could not sleep. Already the sky in the east was pale; the moon low, part-covered with cloud. Ferdie had turned on his back. Georgie thought, Ferdie doesn't know and it's the first time it's been like that. Then she fell asleep, in the manner of entering a wasteland where nothing lived.

Once she awoke long enough to go over it again, remembering against her will every detail . . . at least she had not cut off more of them than she normally bought. Whole strings of them had been piled on Mrs Portwine's table, covered with a muslin cloth. She had moved about carefully. Hot candle wax ran down her hand. Then the shaking had become better as she walked around the kitchen. She had seen the dirty washing-up. She could not avoid seeing it. Placing more candles by the sink, standing them on puddles of hot wax, she had slowly moved the dishes into the warm water. She ran more water down her arms into the basin so that it would make no noise. It took her so long that when she had done it she looked around and, finally, finding half a dozen of the very small sausages, which were free in any case, put them into her bag as well.

It had been difficult going to sleep again, as the events of the night tumbled in her mind. Yet, as strange and frightening as it had been, it was not that which kept her awake so much as the certain knowledge that whichever way she looked at it, in spite of having washed the dirty dishes, she had really stolen the sausages, even the small ones.

It was the first time for her.

She had tried to work it out, thinking: if Mrs Portwine paid a maid to do it, it would have cost ten times, more than ten maybe, what the sausages cost. That would not be using expensive maids with white hats and ironed black dresses, like she had seen serving tea to the laughing ladies in town who had seemed so far away from her as they brushed past. Georgie was working it out using cheap maids: red-knuckled people.

But yet again she told herself, in spite of this, the fact remained that she was now a thief.

In the morning, when Mr Farrants saw the small sausages, Georgie said, "They're for people that goes in regular, and they cost nothing."

"You have 'em. Both of you!" he said. "Always leaving the sassages for me, the pair of you!"

So it was that they too started to eat them, although Georgie often toyed with them on her plate, because of her feelings of guilt. And she was so tired!

She would often doze at odd moments during the day following the night's stealing.

"Really Georgie," said the schoolmistress, "you look as if you are going to fall off the bench!"

"I'm alright miss, thank you miss."

But Ferdie, watching her, knew that she was not.

At home it was worse. The sound of the hissing kettle; the sight of Mr Farrants' head nodding as he sat in his chair; and the wind buffeting at the edge of the roof; all of these things made her sleepy. Ferdie thought what shiny skin and bright eyes she had when she was like this. Sometimes she felt sick with tiredness.

But she could see how much better their home was looking, with all the sausage money being spent on things for the house. And it was not only the sausage money: strangely, Mrs Portwine had started to give her odd cups and plates that were slightly cracked. Almost as if sensing her guilt, she had said, "Take them, child. It is alright, go on. It will make your home nice." Georgie thought, all these good things could go tomorrow. Then where will we be? If I am found out, what will happen?

It did not help matters that by now both she and Ferdie had acquired a taste for the sausages, which happened to be the small ones, but which nonetheless were made with the same delicious meat. How united they seemed at breakfast, all sitting together!

"Very fine," said Mr Farrants one morning in between mouthfuls. "I don't know how she does it." Saying this, he remembered having seen her in the woods, also in the hedgerows, carrying her basket. There were stories that Mrs Portwine mixed in many strange things with her pigmeat.

After Mr Farrants had left for the woods, Ferdie said, "I followed you last time, Georgie. Why didn't you tell me? I came back after you'd gone in, but why did it take so long?"

"I was going to tell you," she said slowly.

"Why did it take so long?"

"I do the dirty dishes."

For a moment Ferdie was quiet. "Then it's not proper stealing is it?"

But Georgie did not answer that. "I'm glad that you know. It's much better that you do."

*　　*　　*

Mr Alistair Fitz-Maurice also liked breakfasts, but his were usually of fried eggs on toast with a slice or two of cold pheas-

ant. He liked the feeling of everything being in place, of
people waiting upon him. Usually he would take the mail
offered to him on a silver plate, and be satisfied with the way
the world was shaping up about him.

On this particular morning a velvet rain fell in between
bouts of sunlight. Birds sang. It had the makings of an
altogether comfortable day. But Mr Fitz-Maurice did not feel
his usual self. He did not open his mail. He sent the toast back
to the kitchen, saying it was overdone.

"Gordon!"

"Yes, Uncle?"

"I have to see the Farrants today and it does not please me
particularly. You can come with me boy, and see how I deal
with estate people and so on. You'd like to come?"

Gordon carefully buttered his toast. "Yes please, Uncle."

"After that we'll shoot rooks eh? What say, boy?" For now
the rooks were just right. Strong enough, they would be able
to leave their nests and claw around the branches, lined up, as
their parents swept beyond the gunshot, wheeling up, taking
the wind. "You would like that Gordon?" he repeated.

"Rather!"

"Rook pie is a fine dish. By the time your parents come back
from China you will know all manner of things about country
life."

"Can I take my gun with me when we see the Farrants?"

"I think not. It's only a small shotgun I know. But after all,"
he added with an effort at humour, "this is not goin' to be an
armed raidin' party. Fellow's complainin' that's all. But I'll
muddle him up, you watch!"

When they arrived at the shed, Georgie said, "Good
morning," and carried on cleaning the pots, flushing as she
did so. Mr Fitz-Maurice stood by the door looking bored and
pale, like his nephew. He was wearing a green satin waistcoat
which suited his complexion very well.

Gordon Buckingham had cut a hazel stick and had ringed
the bark with his pocket-knife. He had gone into the kitchen
and was touching the string of dried mushrooms with the
stick.

"Do not do that, boy," said his uncle. "Now tell me, child,"
– he turned to Georgie – "where d'you heat the water for

cleanin' that pot?"

"On top of the stove, sir."

"Where d'you get the water?"

"From a spring in the woods."

"It is a clear spring?" His voice became richer in tone. He ignored Mr Farrants, who had come in from the garden. "A clear woodland spring! And minnows dartin' hither and thither in the pool? Well Farrants," he added, "at least we know where you get it from. There are people livin' in cities, half their lives spent in shadows and smoke, worryin' about where to get a cup of tea, never touched a flower, cookin' in ramshackle kitchens, bits of pork and so on. Terrible life! Water from a clear woodland spring! Water? Water! If people knew about it they would envy you."

But Mr Farrants merely held open the door to their sitting-room. "If you would care to come in, sir."

Gordon stopped tapping the table with his stick, prepared to follow his uncle. But Mr Farrants put out his arm and shut the door. "Well, we can all hear what is said, can't we?" said Gordon.

"Dad is talking privately with Mr Fitz-Maurice," said Georgie.

Ferdie could not take his eyes away from Gordon, who was still tapping the table and chairs.

She said, "Can't you stop doing that."

"It's the water that is bothering us," Mr Farrants was saying. "There's piped water up to Mrs Portwine's. It's not far."

"The cost from there sir! Farrants, the cost! And there's another thing, I won't have the girl callin' at the cottage. They are very respectable tenants."

"Georgie, come in here for a minute," Mr Farrants called. "No more visits to the cottage . . . understand?"

"And Farrants. You can stay here, don't misunderstand me, but remember it is my wood. Doing a good job, stakes for the estate, pointin' and creosotin'."

"With no money for it," said Mr Farrants.

"Ah, but you cut and sell beansticks and so on, and the boy and the girl take me primroses."

"They're my children!"

"Of course Farrants." His eyes had grown waxy looking. "Of course. And as long as there's no drunkenness you can stay."

"I do not drink," muttered Mr Farrants.

"And no thieving and so on."

"My children, sir," Mr Farrants was now barely able to control his anger as he put a shaking hand on Georgie's head, "do not steal and nor do I!"

"Well of course, I don't doubt it. So you have no need to fear, Farrants. Come along, Gordon."

Ferdie rushed past him to open the door. "Oh dear," he said, "I caught your poor stick."

"You've broken it," said Gordon. "It was on purpose."

"Gordon, come along!" Outside Mr Fitz-Maurice added: "Now we can do a little rook shootin'. Well, are you comin' or not?"

Bending down to the softly clucking hen, Mr Farrants said, "There my lovely!" taking a warm brown egg from her. His nose itched with the smell of feathers from the box. As he passed Georgie, standing at the stove, he rubbed his nose violently again. "Ah, that's better," he said.

Georgie's eyes were red.

To Ferdie he said: "Let's have the broken stick. No sense in leaving it lying around." He opened the stove lid, then looked at them steadily for a moment. "Things'll get better. Mark my words."

Ferdie had seen a young rabbit in the lettuce rows. He ran off, whooping and waving his arms.

"You'll see," Mr Farrants repeated to Georgie.

She thought she might one day tell Mr Fitz-Maurice what it was really like taking water from the spring. But no one talked of it again, in spite of Mr Farrants assurance that things would get better. In fact, she saw her father touch his cap to Mr Fitz-Maurice on the very next occasion.

Nothing seemed to be changing, which in a way was what Georgie wanted. Sometimes a rabbit would come out of the hedge to nibble a lettuce; by the end of the bean row Mr Farrants had stacked cordwood ready for the winter; the ground was littered with orange and yellow marigolds; the main potato crop had started to swell in the earth. And so it seemed to Georgie that everything was happening as usual and was alright. That the journeys to Mrs Portwine's kitchen were another part of her life which could be ignored, which could never threaten the sweet daytime life and end it for ever.

Her blood pounding in her head, she recalled Mr Farrants saying: "My children don't steal!"

She had half-believed it, denying the stealing in talks with Ferdie. "We do a lot of work for those sassages!"

"But Mrs Portwine must know somebody does it," he said. "She must find out, Georgie. It isn't safe anymore."

Georgie tried not to think about it. When she went to the cupboard for her candles she tried not to look at the pots of strawberry jam. When next she was making pastry she said to Ferdie, "We'll have strawberry jam from the special pots. There's no sense in keeping it. It'll go off I expect."

"We've got plum jam," he said, "and there's jam from the old lady."

"We'll have the strawberry."

"There's blackberry." His voice quivered.

As she put the jam back she said quietly so that Ferdie would not hear: "Yes, I'm a thief. Our mum would have told me. There's no mistake about it."

But she was unable to stop. She went on stealing.

On the black nights with no shadows cast, nor even stars showing, she and Ferdie could not see the outline of Mr Fitz-Maurice's mansion against the skyline. But when they did see it they knew he was there, asleep. They could imagine Gordon in his four-poster in the guest room, and the butler in his bed and the cat asleep on the pantry table. And as they fumbled their way to Mrs Portwine's kitchen, when there was no outline, they could imagine Mr Fitz-Maurice at the next corner instead; or if it was wet, Gordon Buckingham standing under an umbrella as black as everything else. Georgie could imagine it very well. Stepping forward, Mr Fitz-Maurice saying: "Ah the Farrants children? Ah!" Unable to see his face properly, then his green satin waistcoat shining for a moment as he lit a cigar.

"They must know," said Ferdie.

"Who?" Georgie was startled out of her dream.

"Mr and Mrs Portwine of course."

"But they haven't found out," she said, "and if we're careful they won't."

*   *   *

Mr Farrants might have noticed that the children looked tired and careworn, had he been free of worries himself. But he was not.

Tying up the beansticks one afternoon, he spoke aloud. The burst of words surprised him. He looked about him to make sure he had not been heard. Of course he had not! For both Georgie and Ferdie were in the town with their kindling and bunches of wild flowers.

Occasionally he had told them, had he not, how well the house looked. It seemed to him that they had worked so hard and sold their kindling at such good prices that over the months they had almost turned the hut into a place as pleasant as the cottage used to be. He groaned. Knowing for sure that no one could hear him, the nearest people being Mr and Mrs Portwine at least a mile down the road, he said again, but louder: "Oh Lord, I am ashamed of my lust for sassages!"

For the way Mr Farrants saw it was that if he ate more vegetables from the garden instead of forever building up supplies to guard against a rainy day as Mrs Farrants had urged him to do, if only he could eat more of such things, instead of letting most of them rot, he could then put the sausage money aside for helping Georgie and Ferdie in their efforts to furnish the hut.

Once or twice, when the children were at school, Mr Farrants had eaten at Mrs Portwine's because, he told himself, "of the cold weather". But today it was warm and summery and there was no excuse for a visit, other than his passion for sausages, of which he was now so deeply ashamed.

He hesitated, fumbling in his pocket as if searching for something, in case he was seen standing outside not knowing what to do. The meaty smells drifted through the half-open door. For a while he stood there, his nose moving, scenting; a little moist it seemed, like the nose of a woodland deer sniffing in the wind.

As he walked homewards after his feed, now satisfied but ashamed, he made up his mind about sausages.

"Georgie," he said later, "with things looking so nice already in our home, the least I can do is to help by giving you the sassage money for a while, towards things for the house. And in that time," he said, "I won't eat no sausages. Not if Mrs Portwine herself brings a basketful here for nothing, I won't."

For several meals Mr Farrants ate carrots, cabbage and potatoes, with a pat of melting butter and pepper and salt, telling Georgie once that there was nothing to beat it, but with Mrs Portwine down the road Georgie knew that this was not so. Then sometimes he had partridge also, which he first plucked and dressed for Georgie, who then did not mind handling it as she was not reminded of the live partridge crouching in the grass of the fields.

He had to be careful what he took, Georgie knew that. Mr Fitz-Maurice let him have rabbits, but taking other things from the fields and woods was different. Georgie knew what would happen if they were caught. She wondered about it, often. Certainly if Mr Fitz-Maurice walked in one day, without knocking, as was the case usually, saying "Ah Farrants", looking at the partridge meat, she knew what would happen to them all. She also understood that the bird tasted all the better for being taken. Unlike sausage stealing, the evil of which she could understand, this kind of stealing was different.

For a while at least, she did not go to Mrs Portwine's in the night.

3

The Note

Mrs Portwine owned a pony and trap, and before driving off she would usually powder her nose and then rummage in her bag for scent as if that was quite the proper thing to do. Sometimes she would pause to look at some faded photographs, damaged and reddened where they had been in contact with make-up: photographs of her and Mr Portwine when they were newly married. Her lips had been full and firm then, not shaky as they sometimes were now, or pursed in thought, or widened like a frog's in stubbornness.

One windy day, soon after Mr Farrants had stopped eating sausages, she parked her pony and trap outside his home. Samantha, who had a plait of black hair and deep blue eyes which never seemed fully open, sat with her back to her mother.

Mrs Portwine was shouting at Georgie, who had come out to see what they wanted. But because of the noise of the wind shaking the tin roof, and the horse tossing its head and snorting and making the harness jingle, Georgie could not at first understand.

"Well, what do you say?" Mrs Portwine had opened her bag and was examining her nose closely in a make-up mirror.

Samantha said, "Your brother can sit beside me."

Then Georgie fetched Ferdie. "Mrs Portwine wants to take us for a trap ride."

"Why?"

"I don't know. She's never done it before. I want to go, but it is strange all the same."

They turned right, past the café, away from the direction of the town, down lanes that crossed with others high up on hedge-covered hillocks, with no direction signs to be seen. At one crossroad Georgie did see a sign, but she could not read it. In fact all it said was BROWN EGGS.

It was as if all the smells of the cut grasses in the fields, the poppies with their bitter smell, and cow stalls and garden flowers were swirling in the wind. The horse was galloping so fast that occasionally Mrs Portwine, her face set and unsmiling, would pull at the reins, shouting: "Whoa there! Whoa!" They saw a mixed flock of crows and starlings hovering in the strong wind, motionless as they faced it, then turning and disappearing at great speed over a rise in the ground.

Samantha sometimes looked at Ferdie. Her head shook, but whether it was a greeting or whether she was merely being shaken by the lurching trap, Ferdie did not know. So he smiled every time Samantha's head moved like this, to be sure about it.

The lanes were sometimes barely wide enough for the trap, and Georgie anxiously held on to the rail by the side of her seat. They passed Mr Fitz-Maurice's mansion with two stone lions at the gates and she hoped that Gordon had seen them, but no one was in sight. Another garden flashed by, with a peacock on a long lawn, and a child there as well, dressed in white, with its nurse or mother.

When Ferdie got down he looked stiff and held on to the trap wheel to steady himself. Samantha was actually smiling down at him. There was no mistaking it. "Goodbye," she said.

Mrs Portwine looked steadily at Georgie.

"Thank you very much, Mrs Portwine."

She continued to stare at her and Georgie said, "Well come along Ferdie, we'd best go."

Then all of a sudden, smiling so earnestly that the lines on her lips disappeared, Mrs Portwine said, "The pleasure is mine!" and tapped the horse with her stick.

They moved off slowly down the road towards the café, a silvery thread of saliva falling from the horse's mouth right down to the ground.

*   *   *

On that very same day, purely by chance, Mr Farrants returned to his sausage-eating habits. So, soon after that, the children were back again in Mrs Portwine's kitchen.

Ferdie was pointing to a plate, set aside from the others, which was clean except for a patch of dried mustard. Next to it was a note, written in capital letters.

At least Georgie could recognize her own name! "It's for us, I'm sure it is. I think we should go now, Ferdie."

"What about the washing up?"

"We don't have to. Come on, I said!"

It was not until they got home that Ferdie realised he still carried the note in his hand.

Lighting a candle, Georgie tried again to make out more of the words but could not. Suddenly she felt anger that they were not like the other children. If they had piped water, or could live in somewhere like the cottage again, or if Mrs Farrants could be alive and with them, they would not smell, and then they would not be put on their own bench at school, making it difficult to learn. Then Georgie had an idea. "We will take it to the vicar. Whatever it says, he will not tell anyone but us."

"Why?"

"Because it's to do with the way they are in the Church. They would not go to the police with it."

She dreaded seeing Mrs Portwine again and being asked for another trap ride, in case it was she who had written the note. But she knew she had to find out what it said.

The children started to walk towards the vicarage at the same time as Miss Minnie Maynard was cycling there from another direction.

She was riding along the hummocky lanes, going at great speed, then puffing up the sudden hills, often pausing and looking at the road below, where she could see the Portwine's café and the town beyond. There were several carts and lorries outside the café, looking no bigger than her thumb.

The vicar had said Mrs Portwine would be at the vicarage for afternoon tea and would she like to come too. Bucket, cloth, silver polish, tea and lumps of sugar were all propped in the creaky willow basket strapped to the back of her bicycle. But she was passing all the people she cleaned for, on her way to tea at the vicarage no less!

She had poor rough hands, with scraggy red skin. This was due to helping people, as the vicar put it. Although the doctor

She was cycling among the hummocky lanes.

directed Miss Minnie to some of his elderly patients who could not manage housework, it was mainly the vicar who said, "If you need some help, I know the very person!"

When she knocked the vicar said, "Excuse me ladies, I expect that is Mrs Portwine," saying a moment later: "Oh! Miss Minnie, I had quite forgotten!"

Three ladies were seated at a table. The vicar's wife was placing a plate of iced cakes, each wrapped in paper, beside the currant buns and cucumber sandwiches.

"Of course you all know Miss Minnie, who helps so many people."

The ladies stopped talking. There was Sybil Rowe, old Miss Jarvis and Lizzie Clark, with her head bent down, as it was whenever she talked unkindly of people. They nodded, knowing very well that Miss Minnie did housework. Then they started talking again, for a moment their voices like a gathering of seagulls, making their chaotic cries.

Miss Minnie was sitting on the edge of a chair, clasping a currant bun, listening to the vicar thanking her for at least the third time for calling, when there was another knock at the front door. But it was not Mrs Portwine. It was Georgie and Ferdie.

They were asked in and stood awkwardly in front of the ladies. Ferdie held out the piece of paper with the message.

"Well, what is it?" asked the vicar. "What can I do for you?"

He felt that perhaps they should not be there, since clearly the only person who would be willing to share tea and cakes, or the brown bread and cucumber, was Miss Minnie, judging by the looks on the others' faces.

"I expect you would like to come into the kitchen." There he turned to his wife, who was cutting more cucumber sandwiches. "Look after the ladies my dear. I shall not be long."

She glanced at the children, opened the kitchen back door and smiled at them as she left to join the ladies. Georgie knew very well why she had done that, although all she could smell was the cut cumber and that was pleasant enough.

"Please sir," said Georgie, "we can't read." And she gave him the note.

"Oh I see!" He smiled.

She had never been as close to him as this before and was surprised at the size of his ears.

He read the note again and, crossing his hands on his lap, said, "Tell me about it."

"It was next to a plate with mustard on it. And that's all," said Georgie, looking hard at her brother.

"You're Mr Farrants' children, aren't you? I saw you after your mother died."

"What does it say?" said Georgie, surprising herself at her rudeness.

"I must call and see you," the vicar replied, then, seeing the puzzled look on her face, added: "It says, 'This simply won't do!' and", he went on, "I will call and see you! If you are having difficulty with housework I know the very person."

"Thank you," said Georgie, "but we can manage very well."

"Not according to the note. And fancy your father not knowing you can't read! But then I've known of other children just like you who would not admit to it, even to their parents. Best be open with him my dears."

"We will," said Georgie.

"Anyway, writing notes is not as good as having it out. I must tell your father."

"I wouldn't," said Georgie. "It's 'is habit to leave notes when he goes off to the woods."

"And Miss Minnie would, I am sure, oblige with some help in return for fresh vegetables," he continued. "Your father's garden always looks so nice from the road."

Then he went to the dresser. His back was half turned. But Georgie, who was standing behind him ready to leave, could see with some surprise what he was doing.

"I must now go," he said, pausing to slyly clean his lips, "back to the ladies."

Again Georgie saw him furtively help himself to another cold sausage from a plate on which there was a little mustard. He held the sausage, biting into it sharply and pulling. Georgie thought, that's the sound of sassage skin, I know it.

He put the plate in the dresser drawer, which was marked "Sermons" and turned to face the children. His face was shining, his eyes beady. "Yes, I must return to the ladies. You may go this way if you like," he said, pointing to the back

He held the sausage, biting into it sharply.

door. "I will tell Miss Minnie. Yes, I will make a point of it."

*   *   *

And the very next day, having seen her as he had promised, he called at Mr Farrants', astonishing him by saying straight away: "I quite agree with you, of course it won't do! How can you do it without proper running water. You do not have running water?"

"We do not, sir," said Mr Farrants.

"It's a disgrace. Of course it won't do!" Clasping his hands he repeated: "It simply won't do."

"I wish you'd tell that to Mr Fitz-Maurice," said Mr Farrants quietly, referring to the lack of piped water.

It started to rain. Large drops fell on to the tin roof, followed by a silence. The vicar sniffed.

"It's the creosote tank hotting up," said Mr Farrants, "and the smoke, it's not very convenient as you might say."

Outside the hut, the air was full of the sound of birds. Pigeons rose in sudden flight against a sky turned black with the oncoming storm.

"You were quite right to say 'it won't do', but no one, let alone children, could be expected . . . " but the vicar's words had been drowned by the din of heavy rain.

Georgie and Ferdie rushed in open-mouthed.

"Rub yourselves down," shouted Mr Farrants, "and if the kettle's hot perhaps the vicar . . . Georgie, some cake!"

The vicar was watching Ferdie, who was breathing in deeply.

Mr Farrants explained: "They do it," he said, "it's the creosote. Breathing it in is good for the chest."

Georgie was fidgeting, worried about the note. Seeing that the vicar had not yet helped himself to cake, she went into the kitchen saying to herself: "Please do not talk about the note. Talk about anything but not the note!" She put some cold sausage on a plate. Returning, she said to the vicar: "Would you like a sassage?"

He raised his voice far more than was necessary to make himself heard above the rain, which was now falling steadily, almost shouting: "I must go!" as if the devil himself, who knew his weakness, was tempting him. "I must go! Not good enough. I promise you I will speak to Mr Fitz-Maurice about it."

As he was leaving a puddle of rainwater suddenly appeared on the floor near Mr Farrants' armchair. Georgie stood in front of it, hoping he would not see it; no longer worried about the note, she was instead deeply and suddenly ashamed of the place in which they lived, and that was in spite of the small ornaments and hangings and furnishings they had been able to buy of late because of their visits to Mrs Portwine's kitchen.

"I would not mind a bit of cold sassage myself," said Mr Farrants after the vicar had gone. "But what beats me," he went on after a moment, "is why the vicar should have known I said 'it simply won't do'. I said as much to Mr Fitz-Maurice, in a manner of speaking I did at least."

"You said as good as that," Georgie assured him quickly.

"'Twas passed on I expect."

"That's right, Dad." A warmth and certainty filled her. It's alright now, she thought, I am never going to be found out!

But later Ferdie said, "Can't we stop it, Georgie? Mrs Portwine knows. She must know it's us."

"No she mustn't," said Georgie slowly. "It could have been Mr Portwine who wrote it."

"Or Samantha."

"She wouldn't use words like that."

But she secretly thought it was Mrs Portwine. It was the way she looked at Georgie whenever they met. It was the way her eyes had lingered on her, making Georgie feel uncomfortable, Mrs Portwine fumbling in her bag for her powder and scent, looking into the glass, moving her chin from side to side, head up, stretching the old neck skin to look like a young woman, then saying to Georgie: "You must come out for a trap ride today." Whisking past the last trusses of summer berries with Mrs Portwine! It has to be her, Georgie thought.

She worried about it for days. And it was only the business of the stews that finally took her mind off it.

Miss Minnie had arranged to call regularly at the hut to prepare meals. She had told the children to lift a few carrots and onions from the garden. "But not too many. From what I've heard, I fancy he's had enough of that."

She was adding various flavourings when Georgie said, "He'll never eat it, miss. He never will. In fact he hasn't had no stew since our mum made it."

"I hope he will eat it," said Miss Minnie quietly.

"Well 'e won't!"

But he did. She gave Mr Farrants more. Not the vegetables, but more meat, carefully selecting it, swirling the ladle around in the mist that still arose from the pot, searching for the pieces of it.

She came regularly on the Saturdays that followed and Georgie did not even seem to notice that Mrs Portwine's trap rides were not so regular, or to miss them, because of the pleasure of sitting down at table again like a proper family.

4

A Secret No Longer

The Member of Parliament was an elderly gentleman with transparent-looking hands and a high-pitched laugh. "I said, you have a splendid place here, Fitz-Maurice."

"Kind of you to say so."

"I remember back in – oh, I don't know exactly. My father brought me here, to a splendid party like this. I was as boy you know, extraordinary, that."

"I would like you to meet General Sir Whyke and Lady de Bonneville, at present living on my estate," said Mr Fitz-Maurice, anxious not to hear details of the M.P.'s early life yet again, and in his rather odd way of putting things.

Spitting joints of meat were being carried to the servery. On the sideboard were puddings and trifles at which, earlier, Gordon had gazed longingly.

He was outside when the gong sounded, hiding behind a rose bush with huge yellow flowers which looked colourless in the moonlight. He had sneaked out there to smoke a cigar, but now wished that he had not because of a gathering feeling in his stomach. As he thought of the trifles he felt worse.

He looked up at the sky, milky with starlight, thinking of himself as Gordon de Buckingham, a sort of black knight with plumes and money and good fortune. It was the sort of thing, this thinking, that he found more exciting than looking at an atlas or handling his uncle's stamp collection.

"Ah, there you are boy!"

"Yes Uncle." His hair was neatly brushed, his face paler than usual, contrasting with his dark-blue velvet suit.

Lady Eunice glanced across the table at him, a table laden with glasses and flowers and food, and bowls with glass fishes bobbing about into which guests could dip their fingers before using their napkins. She said to the Member of

Parliament: "A nice boy, such a nice boy that is."

"What say?"

"I said how nice," she replied, giving up.

"Exactly so."

At the end of the table the General was leaning towards Mr Fitz-Maurice. "That M.P. Odd fellow. Deaf and all that. Seems a bit past it to me."

"He retires from politics next month."

"Then why don't you stand for it? Put your name up. Get votes. Be a Member of Parliament!"

"You think so?" And the idea would not leave Mr Fitz-Maurice. He did not even notice Gordon walk quickly from the room as the cream-topped trifles were put on the table.

"The local people respect you and all that? You get on with your estate workers? It's important that you do."

"Well there *is* a person who keeps complainin' and demandin'."

"Yes, but by getting on with them and even doing good things for them, and maybe getting a bit in the local paper about it, people can see what a splendid fellow you are."

"It's Farrants. He's arguin' about where he lives. I cannot stand arguin'. I have been very kind to him, make him no charge. I cannot make head nor tail of it!"

"You do very well," said the General. "I have seen you in argument. Perhaps it is because you find it so upsetting that you do very well at it, although you may not like it. And if you are going into politics there will be a lot of arguing, but not with the voters!"

"I do try to get on with people."

"There's people – our kind, don't you know – and the other sort of people. Must get to know 'em and how they feel. Often said that. Particularly if you're a military man like meself, or a budding politician."

Mr Fitz-Maurice did not have arguments with his servants and people like that. He ate rook pie, roast partridge; had fresh bedsocks every night; drank wine from very old glasses, which, if sold, would have fetched the price of piped water for the Farrants. All of that, with no arguments!

Once during the week, remembering the General's advice, he tried to bring himself to see Mr Farrants, but instead walked on slowly towards Mr and Mrs Portwine's.

Well, here also were some ordinary people whose votes he wanted. Ordinary people: in their gardens, sitting in deckchairs, watching a bee in a sunflower, or something like that, breaking pea pods with grandma; unemployed men, greyish faces, stubbled chins, talking and chuckling, although he could not imagine what they possibly had to chuckle about. The sort of people who picked potatoes in the fields.

"I cannot see him," he muttered, thinking of Farrants. "I cannot stand the fellow for his impudence."

He gazed at the assortment of lorries parked by the café and at a gypsy cart to which a shivering dog was tied, thinking: these are the people, all workin' hard, the ones the General was talkin' about. Only last Sunday the vicar mentioned somethin' about workin' people. "The sweet sleep of a labourin' man!" He stopped, uncertain, twirling his stick. Well, the people did this sort of thing in their time off. The smell from Mrs Portwine's kitchen lingered, spread about him in the motionless air.

He had heard about the sausages.

As a young boy he had stumbled into a bush and further in had seen the little soft eyes of a mother bird. The bird had left the nest. In the hedge centre, where it was brown with unleafed twigs, with hardly any light, he had gazed at then taken the warm blue speckled eggs one after the other, as if he was standing alone in the core of a dream.

So it was all he felt now. All thought of meeting people had gone. If he could find a corner, alone perhaps. There were three carters sitting at a table. But they ignored him. Mrs Portwine stood at the counter. She beheld him in the silence, her nostrils slightly dilated, her breathing quickened, gulping in from the top of her chest, lightly.

She said: "Is there something?"

"It's very homely in here," he replied softly.

Then she knew what he had come in for and she sensed the sinking feeling he had about it all. So in a voice which was a "never hold it against you or mention it again" voice, and pointing to a separate room which was unoccupied, she said, "Would you like some sausages?"

Relaxing over a pot of tea he thought of Mr Farrants and the people whom the general had mentioned. Best thing, he thought, is wait till I'm elected. Need to be liked. Then I'll evict him!

Mrs Portwine hovered, feeling the skin on her neck, ready to powder it.

Drumming his fingers on the table, he thought, with a little burst of pleasure: after that, not before, I'll catch him poachin'.

"Was it to your liking?"

"Oh yes, Mrs Portwine. Must come again. I must say, very tasty. Standin' for Parliament. Best sausages I've ever had. Might I ask what d'you put in 'em, eh? Herbs? Seasonin'?"

"Pork mainly. Some beef. Bits and pieces."

"What kind of bits and pieces?"

"Ah!" said Mrs Portwine, smiling, lowering her head to one side in a show of great respectfulness.

After he had gone she grabbed her hand-mirror. She smiled into it, running her fingers down the skin of her neck, saying out loud: "That would be telling. That it certainly would, Mr Fitz-Maurice!"

*   *   *

The rain broke into sudden silver cords down the big trees. The field ditch at the side of Mr Farrants' vegetable patch sang with it.

Gordon and Mr Fitz-Maurice, who was carrying a gun, were about to walk across the fields towards a spinney where it was good to wait for pigeon coming into the cabbage. Now without more to-do they ran towards the Farrants hut, for shelter by the creosote tank.

Georgie too had run for cover from the garden. Then, catching sight of someone standing at the side of the hut, she had walked there to see who it was. In a moment she was joined by Ferdie. Georgie felt most uncomfortable in her wet clothes, stiff and cold with the rain. Ferdie started to move to the back door but Georgie stood motionless. Gordon looked fixedly past his uncle. Mr Fitz-Maurice actually smiled at Georgie. But she just stared, not lowering her eyes or smiling back. Then she turned abruptly and ran inside.

That night Mr Fitz-Maurice had another party but, because

of the flooded roads, half of his guests did not arrive. Sometimes he wondered if he should bother with politics! Also he did not seem to have a way with people. Gordon had seen it: that episode with the Farrants child not smiling back as if she was afraid of him. He could not seem to reach people, and here was the General, with a glass of wine in his hand, telling him as much again.

"Now you take my advice. Go out and meet the people. Get their sympathy. Talk to 'em. Then do a bit of listening."

The next time he went into Mrs Portwine's, he walked in boldly, determined to behave as other people did, ordinary folk that is.

"Will it be sausages?" Mrs Portwine asked softly, smiling.

"Yes it will," he said rather snappishly, "but not on my own."

The tables were full of carters, waving forks and knives about as if they were weapons. There was a smell of tobacco from those who had finished but for their tea. Some guffaws of laughter broke out from one of the tables.

Georgie had seen Mr Fitz-Maurice leave the café.

"Dad, 'e was as near to me as you are now!" she said. "Coming out of the Portwine's. And he smiled again, and that's the second time!"

"I dessay it's on account of his going into politics. And maybe he'll git the sassage habit too, but I know I'm breaking it and that's for sure. And in that regard, it helps with Miss Minnie doing stews on Saturdays."

"I'm sure it does," said Georgie, biting her lip and wishing that she had been as successful in persuading her father to eat stew again.

"Besides, the weather has got too warm agin for sausages." Mr Farrants was evidently pleased with himself as he settled down to boiled vegetables taken from the garden. "There's nothing like this." He smiled.

Except a sausage perhaps, Georgie thought cheekily.

When they had gone to bed she asked Ferdie: "D'you think often about the cottage?"

"I don't remember it as much as you. But things is pretty good, ain't they?"

"It's not just the cottage," she went on, in the middle of a revelation, "it's the time just before the sassages I miss."

"How d'you mean?"

"It was better for us before we started stealing sassages. I wish we didn't, that's all."

"And we're still going to give it up alright?"

"Oh yes we will. Don't worry. And as for the sassages we've got, they'll go bad in this weather if we don't watch it. He seems to be 'aving one of his 'no sassage' turns." Sleepily she thought, then we'll have to dig them in by the carrots, away from the rats.

The answer came to her in an unexpected way the next day. They had gone to peer through the hedge at the cottage, going the field way, across the stubble. As she put her head through, Georgie saw Susan, the General's daughter, standing on the other side, looking as surprised as she was. She said, thinking fast, "We've got some sassages that need using up and we're going to sizzle 'em in the woods. How about it?"

Susan answered, "That would be fun!"

"If you want to come, we'll be by the old beech on the edge of the wood in minutes, after we've been to the 'ut."

As Susan walked into the woods, into the sudden shadows and the ropes of light, she could not stop thinking of Molly Brent-Jones. She could just imagine Molly, who slept next to her in the dormitory, creaming her legs, saying: "Oh how funny. Do tell me Susan. Excruciating! Were you bitten, do tell, Susan."

Well they *might* have fleas, she thought, and it would be advisable that the sausages are well done.

Several times Susan stopped, uncertain about the meeting. Once she was face to face with a young deer. She had so often wanted sausages! Sometimes they had them at school, but they were wretched things, hard and wrinkled in a pool of shiny gravy. Oh yes, she had asked for sausages at home. "We don't eat sausages. You never know what is in them, my dear." And her father had agreed. "You never know what's in 'em!"

Then Susan saw them. The skin by her eyes moved with her heartbeats. Georgie was standing in the hollowed trunk of the beech. "There's room," Georgie called. Susan did not move towards them, but stood fingering her straight gold hair.

Beyond the beech, the wood stopped. Through the trees, across a field, she could see a figure coming towards them, stopping occasionally, bending down. "Who is it?" she asked. "It is alright being here in the wood, isn't it?"

"'Course it is. My dad works in it and it's alright," Georgie said. "It's Mrs Portwine. She collects herbs when no one's looking. It's for her sassages. For 'er sake we'll not let on we're here!"

"She must be a funny lady."

"It's just that she likes to keep it secret what she puts in 'em."

"Are they nice?"

"You'll see."

Mrs Portwine, unsuspecting, came nearer the edge of the wood. Susan squeezed into the bole, where she could not be seen, squatting on the leaves and last year's beech husks. Ferdie was looking at her furtively, sniffing with pleasure and then pretending he had some trouble with his nose.

"She'll go away in a minute," said Georgie. But she came closer.

Susan thought, oh dear, whatever shall I say.

There was the noise of a branch scraping against another as it moved in the breeze. Ferdie was scratching his leg. A pheasant was coming out of the field ahead of Mrs Portwine, taking cover in the long grass by the wood's edge, resting at the end of each short run and making a noise like a chicken when it is comfortable and contented.

Now it was in the wood, not far from them. They squatted motionless, watching Mrs Portwine. Ferdie had stopped scratching. Georgie thought, stupidly, any moment now and she'll bring out her mirror and powder her nose.

She was looking intently into the wood, but not in their direction. Then she bent down to her herb bag and took out a small cross-bow. It was over in a flash. She moved at great speed into the wood, stuffed the pheasant into the bag and started off across the field.

Ferdie said, "Cor, did you see that?"

Mrs Portwine's figure got smaller as she went across the field, stooping occasionally to collect a herb. Sometimes her figure seemed to wobble and bend because of a ground-mist

Mrs Portwine, unsuspecting, came nearer the edge of the wood.

and the distance involved.

"Well I never," said Susan, "I've never seen anybody do a thing like that before."

"No more've we," said Georgie, lapsing into a way of speaking which Mr Farrants used and which had caused some remarks at school.

They poked hazel sticks down the middle of the sausages, and held them over the glowing fire. "This is fun. I never do anything like this," Susan said. "Well you could", Ferdie replied in a low voice, "if you came to the woods again."

For a while there was silence. Occasionally the embers flared up, the flames turning yellow as the fat ran out.

Staring into the fire, Susan said, "Mrs Portwine was poaching that pheasant from Mr Fitz-Maurice. It belongs to him."

"You won't tell no one?"

"No, I won't, Georgie. In any case I don't think poaching is quite as bad, although it's stealing all the same. And no, I won't tell anyone." She looked steadily at Georgie. She wondered what Molly Brent-Jones would make of it all. She might even stop creaming her legs!

The sausages had split, the edges were black and crisp. Georgie said, taking Ferdie by surprise, "We stole them. We steal 'em regular from Mrs Portwine's kitchen, don't we Ferdie."

He nodded, glancing from one to the other, alert, waiting to back up Georgie.

"And we washes up," she said, adding in a dry voice, "don't we Ferdie."

"Always."

Georgie's face was flushed. She clenched her hands. "And I'm glad I told you, d'you hear that? Don't eat your sassage if you don't want."

"I didn't say that," Susan said quietly.

"You know where it comes from!"

A little fat fell on the fire but did not flame up, making only a puff of blue smoke which disappeared into Susan's gold hair. She said, "I could do with another."

Ferdie fetched her another hazel stick. "Keep it away from the flames."

Then they told her more about it. Why they needed the

money for their home that Mr Farrants thought was being spent on sausages. Later Georgie said, "And of course they painted your cottage up after we left."

"And took the old bath out," said Ferdie.

"My parents think it is a very nice place," she said quietly, looking at the ground.

"It's got a nice pantry. You been in it?"

"Yes," she said. Then breaking the silence: "*Your* place is alright, from what you say it seems to be so."

Ferdie looked at her, nodding in agreement, glad that Georgie had stopped talking. "It's pretty good. Considerin'."

When they arrived back at the shed, Samantha Portwine was there. "I want to talk to you, shall I come in? Look, I know about the sausages – what you do, stealing them. And I want to talk to you about it."

Ferdie became as still as a dead mouse.

"What are those?" Samantha asked, looking at the ceiling.

"Dried mushrooms," replied Georgie in a low voice.

Samantha held out a bag of aniseed balls. Ferdie, whose mouth had gone dry, took one.

Georgie said, "What d'you mean?"

"It's funny, I haven't been here before." Then Samantha went on: "My parents won't let me read romances. So I read when it is really late, after they have gone to sleep."

"It's not to do with us," muttered Ferdie.

"I saw you the first time. Through a hole in the floor."

"Maybe it weren't us."

But Georgie said, "We aren't doing it no more. Our dad's breaking the habit."

"You should see him," Ferdie said, "with 'is vegetables, and Saturday stews."

"And we've enough things," added Georgie. "Look at it! China, ornaments, curtains. It wasn't like this at all, and it's so because of our dad's sassage money what went astray."

They told her everything.

Georgie paused, pressing her hands together. "We've talked about it a lot. About stopping. Ferdie's often said we've got to stop and I've said the same. Only this time we've really stopped."

"We 'ave."

"Helped by our dad breaking the habit," she added to fill the silence.

"We ate the last ones in the woods."

"We've stopped! And we've not been taking them regular like we did."

"That's it," said Samantha, "that's the trouble! You see, I told my mum that I had done the extra washing up. Every time I told her it was me."

"You must have had a reason for saying that."

"I always hated doing it. But although she said how pleased she was I didn't get much more pocket money. I could have bought a lot more books: that's what I expected. All that washing up and all I got was a shilling!"

"But you didn't do it!"

"I do now," said Samantha. "My mother said I could not possibly stop once I started. But it was you who had stopped, and look at the mess I'm in because of it. So you must go on with it." She added: "Or I will tell my parents."

But Georgie only said she would think about it.

"And you can buy me some more romances. I'll tell you where. It's a funny sort of shop. He comes into the café sometimes, and if you buy them he won't know who they are really for."

"Why can't you buy them?"

"Well, I do sometimes, but Mr Gould, that's his name, is always saying that one day, because he knows I'm forbidden, he'll tell my dad."

"What are they about?" asked Ferdie.

"We're having nothing to do with it," Georgie said.

"Oh yes you are! It'll be with my money of course." Samantha paused. "I don't mean to be beastly, but we can look after each other."

"What are you doing for us?" he asked.

"Why . . . I'm keeping quiet about you!"

"They're not to know," said Georgie. "Who will believe you anyway?"

"I've got a witness. My cousin saw you one night. She will make a statement."

"Then we'd best go on with it," Georgie said. Her hands and legs felt limp.

Samantha did not see the hooded look her mother gave her as she left.

Afterwards she said,"I should have asked her if she wrote that message."

"I shouldn't bother yourself," Ferdie sighed. "It stands to reason, doesn't it."

So they washed up once a week and often took sausages, which they cooked in the woods. Sometimes it was with Susan. And on Saturdays they called at Mr Gould's bookshop. The first time they saw him he was eating bacon sandwiches.

"Can we 'ave a look?" Georgie asked. "It's romances we're after."

"Over there," he said, pointing to some shelves, "sixpence, or tuppence second-hand." The bacon smelled very nice indeed. "And mind, I can see all around the shop."

As they had left Georgie said, "It's better now that Samantha knows. Because if we do get caught by Mrs Portwine we'll tell 'er everything just as it is. Getting the books proves it, about Samantha twisting our arms, I mean. It wouldn't look so bad for us."

That evening Mr Farrants' eyes looked distant and narrowed, a little ferrety, as he sat down in front of his plate of vegetables and his pat of butter and salt and pepper.

"It looks ever so nice, Dad," said Georgie, remarking to Ferdie afterwards: "It won't be long 'afore he takes to 'is sassages ag'in."

"Well, at least it won't be proper stealing anymore."

Certain now that this was so, Ferdie and Georgie continued to take a few sausages after their weekly visits, often sharing them with Susan over a wood fire.

And each morning following one of their visits Samantha would smile at her mother as if to say, "once again I've done it!" She often wondered whether to ask for more pocket-money but decided not to. Once she did say, "I hope it's all done nicely enough?"

"Oh yes!" said Mrs Portwine.

Samantha did not see the hooded look her mother gave her as she left: the mouth puckering, the eyes unblinking, flecked with shadows and images like an eagle's eyes, with a preying creature's peace of mind in between meals of rabbits and suchlike.

5

Mr Portwine in Trouble

Mrs Portwine had decided to take a few days' holiday, but on her own because it was difficult, running a café, to do otherwise. She was in a tea shop by the seafront, wearing a fur coat, and a hat the colour of young rooks, looking at the card she had just bought for Mr Portwine. Feeling as warm as toast, with her coat smelling of lavender water, she thought idly about what to write.

Away from the sausages at last! Well, Mr Portwine could manage by himself for a change. She had another coffee, ordered a cake, noticed water oozing from a valve on a radiator and then hissing as it turned into steam. A pink and black car drove by. Such elegance everywhere! Then feebly she wondered again about what to write to Mr Portwine.

She powdered her nose. Some more people had come in, ordering coffee and cakes. The coffee was ground for each customer, filling the café with its aroma. There were no meaty smells. Then she saw the waitress carry a dish of sandwiches to the next table. Brown bread, cut thinly. *Cucumber* sandwiches! She tried again to think of what to say to Mr Portwine. What shall I write, she thought mockingly, shall I write: "Do you remember the cucumber sandwiches, how we met? Spilling a plateful of them in my lap. The romance!"

For a long time she sat looking out of the window, at times at the sea, wafered with silver and untroubled. Then she picked up her pen, trying it first on the back of an old envelope to make sure the ink was running properly. She wrote in large letters, filling the space: "Having nice and most enjoyable rest." Then she sat wondering how Mr Portwine and Samantha would be managing without her.

* * *

In fact Samantha liked being behind the counter on her own, calling out the orders to her father. "With mustard?" she would say to a customer. "Well done? Everything alright?" Just like her mother. "Just a moment please," she would say if someone pushed ahead out of turn.

But Samantha's pleasure was spoiled. Although the Farrants still did the washing-up one night a week as they had been doing for a long time, Samantha now had to do the washing-up on all the other nights, due to Mrs Portwine's absence. So she wrote a letter to herself using her left hand to make it look different. It made the muscles in her arm ache so it was a short letter. "If you want me to give evidence to the police I will. Your cousin, Felicity."

"There," she said to Georgie, "I can hardly stop her. She wants to get you into trouble. But I don't particularly."

Georgie looked at the letter, flushing.

"Oh, of course. I'll read it for you."

"Perhaps I don't care any more."

"Oh yes you do! You must!" said Samantha. "And until my mother comes back next week you must do the washing-up on all the other nights as well."

Mrs Portwine's card arrived the next morning.

In the afternoon Mr Portwine went into town and bought a postcard to send to her. After this, he said to himself, I will have a pot of tea somewhere. But he could not think what to say. A pot of tea! The memory of that ridiculous accident with the cucumber sandwiches came flooding to him. Smiling, trembling a little, he rubbed his eye which troubled him. He was about to write, "Look forward to your safe return," when he realised it was selfish to want her to return so soon. Was she not enjoying herself? But then equally, did he not want her back? He wrote in his normal hand, because it was a small card: "Having good weather at this end. How is it at your end?" When he got back he tried to take an afternoon nap, but could not, thinking of Mrs Portwine and the early days.

That night he slept fitfully, overtired. Then, putting on his dressing gown, he decided to get up and make himself a hot drink. "It's no good," he said, "no good at all. I cannot sleep!" It was four o'clock in the morning. There was, as yet, no dawn light.

Downstairs, Georgie whispered, "Did you hear something?"

"No." Ferdie was rocking on his feet with his eyes nearly closed.

"We've done it now," Georgie said, "come on!"

"Shall we take some sassages?"

"No, we'd best go, Ferdie. I'm sure there was a noise."

"What if Susan wants some?"

"Oh alright!"

As they returned home in silence the cold night air blew leaves into their faces, great flurries of them. The potato stalks in the field were brown and lying flat, the furrows now standing out clearly in the moonlight. Georgie was thinking, I do not want to think about running anymore. When they had decided about an escape route, it was Ferdie who had understood that they would have a better chance than an adult running across this sort of field.

Georgie said, "I think we might tell Mrs Portwine when she comes back."

But always it was the same problem: she and Ferdie knew that if they admitted stealing Mr Fitz-Maurice would have them driven off the land. He had threatened that sort of thing several times.

*   *   *

Down at the police station Sergeant "Bunny" Wheeler, so nicknamed because of his soft rabbity looking moustache, was lighting the gas under the kettle and blowing into his cupped hands.

He had told P.C. White, who had a touch of flu, to rest in one of the cells, but as there was no trouble in the town, he was not overworked. The only call had been from a lady who said she had locked herself out of her flat.

As the tea brewed in the pot, he reflected, as he often did, on the strange ways of some people. He had just decided to open

He remembered it all, looking through a gingerly opened door.

a can of baked beans, which would have gone very well with a thick slice of bread and a cup of tea, when the phone rang.

It was not long after four o'clock in the morning.

Looking back on it, Mr Portwine often wished he had spoken to the children before calling the police. How different it would have all been! After Georgie and Ferdie had left he had noticed odd things because of his excited state as he walked about the kitchen wondering what to do. He remembered it all, looking through a gingerly opened door: the candlelight on Georgie's face as she turned to look into the gloom towards him; Ferdie taking the sausages – a least a pound! Then after they had gone, opening the back door and watching their figures gradually disappear, crusted with moonlight. He had nearly called them.

Mr Portwine had not known what to do. He walked about the kitchen noticing everything. The squeak from the back door had started again. He must get it oiled. The water was dripping out of the overflow pipe. "Thou shalt not steal!" He even noticed that the dishes stacked up on the draining board were warm.

He put on an overcoat to stop the shivering, then he had telephoned the police.

Sergeant Wheeler left his constable in the cell. It took him twenty minutes to get there on his bicycle.

"We'll go along, sir, shall we?" he said, "I can take your statement later, after I have apprehended them. Nothing to prove it, is there, sir, if they deny it? You should have at least made yourself known, sir."

"I couldn't believe my eyes, Sergeant. I was dumbfounded. They are only children! I had to call you, did I not?"

"You're quite right, sir. Quite right. We can't have that sort of thing, can we."

"No we cannot, of course. Perhaps a caution, a word from you will do?"

Sergeant Wheeler thought, now why do some people call the police and spend all their time wishing they had not. He said, "Best be getting along, sir."

As they neared the hut, the leaves from the nearby wood flurried and brushed into Mr Portwine's face. He thought, they were children, perhaps hungery. But he only said, "They are thieves, whichever way you look at it."

"I'm afraid you're quite right, sir." the sergeant replied, shining his torch at the hut. "They will have to be apprehended. As I said, it is a pity you did not make yourself known."

"Perhaps I dreamed it, Sergeant."

"Let's see if they admit it or not."

Georgie slept. But Ferdie was still half-awake and saw Mr Farrants bending over her bed, saying in a dry voice, clearing his throat: "Come on, Georgie!"

"What is it, Dad?" Now she was sitting upright. The lamplight was streaming in from the sitting-room. She could see two figures. One was Mr Portwine, of that she was sure!

"Best get dressed," said Mr Farrants, "and you too," – he turned to Ferdie.

Georgie was taken over by a sudden fit of trembling. Mr Farrants had joined the others and she could get no answer from him. Usually, at this hour, in the uncertain light of dawn, the rabbits would come in to the garden to eat some of the vegetables, but the lights in the hut and the raised voice of Mr Farrants made them uncertain. All of them, except an old buck rabbit, went back to the woods.

The children's statement took a long time. Often Mr Farrants would get up and look out of the window, now and then shaking his head. The pigeons were coming out of the woods, silhouetted black in the pale morning sky. The statement was at last written out to everyone's satisfaction. Sergeant Wheeler read it out. Because of their age Mr Farrants also had to put his mark on it, and again (it was a large cross) against some words in particular which said the statement had been taken of their own free will.

"You'll have to wait and see what the Superintendent says.

"Will it be prison?" Georgie said.

"If you go on doing things like that, one day, miss, it will be for sure! Now Mr Farrants," he went on, "bring them to the station later this morning and we'll see what the Superintendent says."

By the time the sergeant returned to the station it was near the end of his shift. He eyed the can of beans, thinking: now why should such nice children – and they were nice children

– do such a thing? Deep in thought he sauntered into the yard
and took from his cycle bag a parcel containing the sausages.
He wrote out a label and tied it to the parcel. "Police exhibit.
Stolen sausages. Farrants". He opened the can of beans, then
lit the gas under the frying pan. He also emptied the old tea,
which had been brewing away since Mr Portwine's call, and
made a fresh pot.

He read the children's statement. They had admitted to it, at
least once a week since the spring. That was a lot of sausages,
and the motive had been to take their father's sausage money
to buy other things for the house. It all seemed clear enough.
He glanced at Mr Portwine's statement. If it went to Juvenile
Court he would be a difficult witness, he could see that. "Well,
Your Honour, I did not want the police to bring a charge, I was
not sure . . . " and so on. "I watched the children take the
sausages. They are known to me as the Farrants children. I
went to the back door after they had gone. I noticed that the
plates were warm. I noticed that the overflow was dripping. I
noticed that there was a bright moon. I made some cocoa."
The Superintendent would not like a statement like that. All
higgle-de-piggeldy.

Without really considering too carefully the full importance
of what he was doing, he pressed down the lid of the bean can
and opened the police exhibit. He took just two sausages and
placed them in the pan. "It simply beats me," he muttered,
convincing himself that what he was doing could be called
part of his duty, "how anyone could ruin their lives by stealing ordinary sausages."

*   *   *

An hour or so later, although still early in the morning, Miss
Minnie Maynard was, by good fortune, bicycling past the hut
on her way to work, when she saw Mr Farrants. She braked
abruptly, upsetting some Vim and a bundle of polishing rags
from her front basket. As they both knelt down she studied
his pale face and eyes reddened with lack of sleep.

"How are the children?"

"Having a wash."

"It must be cold in this weather for them. If only Mr Fitz-

Maurice would do something for you." Then she added rather timidly: "Is anything wrong, Mr Farrants?"

He told her. "So they had to git washed all over as it's somebody of importance they'll have to see."

"I understand your reasoning," she said.

When she arrived home after a spell of housework, Miss Minnie cut some thin slices of brown bread and mashed two bananas, to which she added a squeeze of lemon juice and some castor sugar. Then, having neatly wrapped the sandwiches in greaseproof paper, she cycled to the Portwine's and saw Samantha.

"Is your dad in there, dear?"

"He's not very well."

"Well, tell him I wish to have a word," Miss Minnie replied a little sharply.

"Mr Portwine, I want to get into town and, rather than wait for the next bus, I wondered if any of your customers here would give me a lift in?"

He looked over the tables. "There's Jack," he said, "he'll be off soon. I'll talk to him. I expect you'll have to wait ten minutes."

"That will do," said Miss Minnie.

"Have you time for a sausage? Would you like a sausage? We have a few short ones today."

"No, no, no!" said Miss Minnie, half rising from her chair. "I do not want any of them. None of your sassages, do you understand?"

"Well, would you like a cup of tea?"

"Yes, I'd love one." She wondered what she could say to the children. Sometimes it was better to just *do* things for people: to say nothing. For example, Mrs Potter's feet. When she called on her it was no good *saying* how dreadful the aches must be. Much better to fill a bowl with warm water and some mustard powder directly she went into the house, and to give her a smile. So she did the same with the children. When she got to the police station the Farrants family were still waiting outside the Superintendent's office. She handed the sandwiches to Georgie and Ferdie and gave them a smile, saying nothing. She sat down with them, waiting with them, and neither they nor Mr Farrants questioned it.

*   *   *

The first thing Mr Farrants did on their return to the hut was to dig up the carrots and potatoes; then the parsnips, which would have stayed fresh in the ground all winter without spoiling.

"Kip 'em in the frosty ground and they git sweeter," he said as he looked at the heap of parsnips. "Pity we took 'em out."

Within a few days he had given the parsnips and all his beansticks and a sack of cabbages to a carter, who called in at Mrs Portwine's every day, where he regularly ate sausages and thick slices of white bread with mustard.

In return, the carter loaded up the Farrants' possessions ready to take to the new home. Georgie took down the string of dried mushrooms and handed them to him.

"Would you take these? My dad don't eat 'em and nor Miss Minnie: she don't eat 'em as well."

"I daresay," he said smiling, putting them in a pile on the passenger seat. He wiped his hand on his trousers. "Thank you, missy."

The jams and pickles and other things had all been packed on the Saturday after coming back from the police. The wild strawberry jam Georgie put in a cloth bag, gripping it tightly. Both children rode in the back, Mr Farrants in the front. The mushrooms had been put on the floor. The ornaments and even necessary things like cups and a new linen teacloth were now packed into boxes, which had been marked with crosses by Mr Farrants.

"And seeing where the money came from to buy all these knick-knacks, we'll leave 'em unopened," he said.

Before he climbed into the passenger seat Mr Farrants said to them, their eyes darkened with pain, calling them "my dears" for the first time in a while, and with no resentment in his voice: "Well, my dears, 'tis better we leave now of our own free will rather than to be put out by Mr Fitz-Maurice when he comes back from his holidays."

The first thing they did in the new place was to light the boiler fire.

Miss Minnie arrived on her bicycle, with both front and back baskets full, gasping: "Look, I've brought some curtains."

"'Tis kind of you to come here, Miss Minnie. I don't say I don't like it. But it won't do to make a regular thing of it."

"I've no intention of that, Mr Farrants. It's just while you all settle. I'll help you a bit, that's all."

"You 'ave your own life to lead!"

"Now," she said, "I thought I would make a stew. There's a butcher round the corner, I see. And you've got a sack of carrots, I noticed, and tatties and parsnips no doubt."

"I've only a few parsnips. Them's best left in the ground for winter, and would 'ave been if the circumstances had been normal, which", he could not help adding, "they ain't by a long way. The carter's got most of 'em."

"Won't they go all limp? And be no good?" she queried.

"That's 'is funeral." Mr Farrants said with a grin.

"Can I help, Miss Minnie?" Georgie asked.

"You can help put up the curtains. I must say, "she went on, "it's very convenient to the shops. What meat shall I get? Scrag end? Brain? Chitlings? It's all cheap."

"I've a bit put by until I git work," said Mr Farrants. "They haven't for example got a rabbit or a couple of wood pigeons?"

"I'll ask," she said.

Later Mr Farrants contentedly pushed away his plate. Miss Minnie had given the children small helpings because she considered their digestion might still be upset. But they both came back for more.

"I'll help you with the rest of the curtains," she said, "and then I'll be away."

Mr Farrants head was bent slightly as he listened. He held up his hand.

"What is it, Dad?" asked Ferdie.

"Quiet! There! There it is again."

A knocking sound came from upstairs.

"It's only the water in the tank," said Miss Minnie.

"It is," said Mr Farrants. "It is so, I knew it, when I heard it."

As the knocking of the hot water in the pipes came again, Mr Farrants would smile and nod his head.

He had the first bath.

Then Georgie had one. How she had dreamed of this! The gaslight hissed. It glowed into the clouds of steam like an old

moon on the mist of harvest nights. She topped up the bath
with water so hot that it made the tap rattle.

Before she went to bed she put away her pickles, herbs,
jams, and jars of salted beans. She put the other jam under the
bed.

Sleepily she saw the hedges in her mind, and the fields. The
potato field! Running for dear life, although it had never
actually happened. Ferdie grunting as he sped through the
lines of dead potato plants. And she remembered the visit to
the police station. "Your name?" "Georgina, sir." The Inspector had stared at her for a very long time. She was glad she had
given away the dried mushrooms. Although only she liked
them, the pleasure she had seen on the carter's face was well
worth it. For the first time since her mother had died, she
dreamed of her bending down, saying goodnight.

Now Georgie's mouth was slightly open, carved, her
breathing light. There was a trickling from a blocked gutter
pipe, as rain fell steadily. The rows of houses, all of the same
appearance, gleamed dully in the rain from the cast light of the
few gaslamps which were left alight all night on the street
corners. A fox that had slunk in from the surrounding
countryside was sniffing garbage left in the narrow alleyway
linking the backyards. Dimly silhouetted, for there were no
stars showing, two huge gas cylinders towered into the sky,
dwarfing the houses.

Their house was No. 97; the road: Gas Works Road.
Although the reason for being there was a sad one, the fact
was that Mr Farrants and the children, for the first few days at
least, found much in the house to make them happy and
contented.

*   *   *

But the same could not be said of Mrs Portwine, who had now
returned from her holiday.

Her friends sat outside her bedroom while she fitfully
dozed, red-eyed, puffy faced, sometimes threshing her head
from side to side on the pillow.

Miss Hilary Jarvis had brought a jar of dried camomile
flowerheads with her, which she had given to Mr Portwine

before going upstairs. She admired Mrs Portwine and was pleased to have her for a friend. Hilary was short, greyish haired, with a mole on her chin. Of the three, Mr Portwine found her the friendliest. Although she did agree with Mrs Portwine about the cruelty of Mr Portwine, not out of unpleasantness but to maintain her position of friendship. She was often accused of being "soft" by Mrs Portwine. She had a fault of playing with the straps on her handbag, and a weakness for chocolate éclairs filled with fresh cream, lightly dusted with icing sugar.

Mr Portwine came in carrying a tray on which was a large pot of camomile tea and four cups. "Here you are ladies," he said.

Lizzie Clark, with deep brown eyes and head going down as she spoke unkindly, like a bullying seagull walking to food, said: "I think we'll take her cup in, the sight of you might upset her again."

"It is supposed to calm the nerves," Hilary Jarvis said. "Would you like to join us, Mr Portwine?"

"Hilary!" said Lizzie.

"I must carry on downstairs," Mr Portwine said, planning his escape. "The sausage machine needs clearing out, you know. Must be done."

Sybil Rowe was the third friend. "Camomile is wonderful," she said slowly, "it will do her so much good. Calming!"

Oh how relaxed Sybil always is, thought Miss Jarvis as she tore at the strap on her bag. Her wide eyes and yellow hats, that gentle look on her face, the way of saying the "ah" in calming, just like the sounds coming off the hills in lambing time, she mused.

Lizzie Clark went into Mrs Portwine's curtained bedroom, carrying a cup. "My love," the others heard her say, "my love, are you awake?"

Sybil said, "Personally I would not feel as sorry for the Farrants family as Mrs Portwine does. After all, they did steal." Then: "Aaah!" she said as she sipped the tea. "Aaah, this is so nice, isn't it."

After they had left, Mr Portwine tip-toed upstairs. Samantha was not yet back from school. The sausage machine gleamed: the café was quiet and still, and in the front window was a notice which read: "Business as usual tomorrow. We regret any inconvenience caused", and another note pinned on the door for Samantha which said simply: "Use the back".

Mrs Portwine was snoring and each time she did so it seemed to half-waken her, for she started blowing her cheeks out and bringing her teeth together rapidly as if she was trying to catch a piece of sausage. Mr Portwine gazed at her for some time. "I think I will leave her be," he muttered.

What a dreadful scene there had been! It pained him to think of it. He edged back from her, closing the door, escaping it seemed, yet again, from the torrent of words, from the anger. "Oh Henry! Henry! You are a fool! A meddling, mindless fool!" she had screamed. "But stealing is stealing," he had said. "How dare you! Calling the police! Because two children, poor children, living in that awful old hut . . . What d'you think people will say?" "I don't know, dear." "That you're heartless. That I'm heartless. I should have stayed away. For good, maybe!"

As the next few days went by, Samantha never failed to ask her father about Mrs Portwine's health. "Is she any better today?"

"She is sitting up."

But, thought Samantha desperately, not strong enough by half to do the washing-up.

Late at night she tried to read, but she was so tired that often she woke up still holding the book in her hands, the candlelight lurching, the shadows leaping as the flames guttered. Every evening after school she had to wash up. She had seen Georgie once when she had gone into town to the bookshop. She asked her: "Would you go on getting books for me? It's not safe for me."

"No," said Georgie, "I'll not."

"You won't tell anyone you did the washing-up, will you? I mean, Mum would be very upset and she's not well as it is."

"I won't," said Georgie after some thought.

"It could get me into a lot of trouble."

Reading helped Samantha of course. Reading about rich people in motor cars. And they were always good-looking. The places they went to, as well! Rome, Tripoli, Cairo. Riding camels, rescuing ladies from desert Arabs, the sort that the town Arabs would not have approved of either. Or boating down the Thames and a strange man hitting a bee that was about to land on a white arm. Afterwards there would be champagne and church bells and vicars, the girl trembling, mounting the first step to everlasting happiness. It made Samantha forget about the washing-up.

Then as the days passed Mrs Portwine began to take ordinary tea and biscuits. Samantha seemed to be living in another world, so much so that Mr Portwine checked the plates and cutlery, occasionally putting an item to the side. Sometimes he re-washed these himself. He was feeling dispirited. He had heard nothing of the Farrants. Everyone in the village seemed to be ignoring him. It was because of this feeling, which weighed him down, that he produced vast quantities of short sausages, his mind not being on what he was doing. Due to the great quantity involved he decided to take all the skins off and to re-use the meat, rather than give them away as had been the custom.

6

Some Thoroughly Bad Behaviour

It seemed that ever since they had moved it had not stopped raining. The rows of cottages gleamed. The pavements and small front gardens stunk of rain.

Once or twice as the children stood and looked at a particular cottage they would see a face, as pale as a dinner plate, move behind the netting. Doors shut, dogs barked, but these sounds and those of motor cars, whistles and voices, were all partly lost as the rain rushed into drains and gutters.

And because of it, Mr Farrants often finished work early.

"You'll be starting your new school next week," he said one evening, "so gitting to know the place won't do no harm." He was quieter: keeping to himself.

"Dad," Georgie said, "why don't you shout at us or something?"

He took off his boots. "I'll take off these clothes directly. They're wet through."

"Poor Dad."

"Is it alright?" asked Ferdie.

"Sweepin' roads? It ain't exactly in my line of business. But it's a job."

"Dad, if it hadn't been for us . . . " Georgie said.

"Look," said Mr Farrants, as he pushed his shoulders back, stretching, anxious to change his clothes, "'tis the sassages that brought us to this, 'tis true! If I had not been driven by lust for those sassages you wouldn't have done it. I should have bought small things for the house instead."

To break the silence that followed, Ferdie said, "D'you still 'ave your bread and cheese for dinner?"

"Without cookin' it on a shovel under the trees, yes I do." Then, more to Georgie, he said, "But stealing is stealing whatever. And you shouldn't 'ave, but there's no sense in my shouting, is there? And there's another thing, you can't sell flowers from the woods and kindling and things no more."

"Not really," she said.

"So there's pocket-money for the both of you, once a week." He handed them thruppence, just as the door knocker sounded. "As regular as clockwork," he said as Miss Minnie let herself in and started on the vegetables.

"These parsnips are getting limp," she said.

"Best left in the ground. If you can, that is."

"P'raps you should have done," said Miss Minnie. "Left 'em in. Not moved from the 'ut."

Georgie usually helped, but she held back, waiting.

"There's only this room fit to be lived in," she went on, "and all the ornaments and things still packed in boxes, if you'll excuse me for mentioning it."

"They stay where they are," muttered Mr Farrants.

"Shall I prepare the rabbit?" Georgie asked, sensing the difficulty.

"Rabbit?" said Miss Minnie. "I've been given none this week."

"Is it woodpigeon then?" suggested Mr Farrants in a friendlier tone.

"No," said Miss Minnie. "If Georgie and Ferdie can clean the potatoes, I'll pop round the corner to the butchers. A few pence'll do it."

Before the meal had ended, Miss Minnie had told them, waiting for the best moment. Mr Farrants was chewing steadily on the tough meat, unable to disguise his disappointment.

Miss Minnie said, "Well, Mr Fitz-Maurice is back from his holiday."

"Is he? He went to Scotland didn't he?"

"And he's in such a state. Making a dreadful fuss. I should say he's almost stamping up and down."

Mr Farrants put his knife and fork on his plate.

"He says," Miss Minnie went on, "he's threatening to cause trouble with Mr Portwine. Of course, we all know it's not the smells really. He wants to get his own back."

"Smells?"

"Oh, he says it's the tea and sassages. Says all the sassage smells going into the air is spoiling the countryside, and that he'll have the law on him. And what's even worse for them, he's forbidden Mrs Portwine to go on his land anymore, looking for herbs."

"I can't understand."

"Well I can," said Miss Minnie. "More stew?"

"Not directly."

"He's angry at your going. D'you know what he was heard to say to the vicar? 'He was often annoyin',' he said, 'but now that he's gone,' he said, 'I find it very upsetting.'" Miss Minnie carefully mimicked his way of speaking. "And I'll tell you what," she wagged her finger, "he's having to think of paying someone a proper wage for doing all the things you've been doing, just for the privilege of being allowed to cut a few beansticks and for letting you live in an old shed."

"Home," said Mr Farrants.

"Well then, so it was," she replied, "and still could be. Now, why don't you go back, on conditions."

"I'll make up my mind on that."

"The conditions being", went on Miss Minnie, "a proper wage and running water."

"He'll never do it!"

"I'm sure he will. I know it. Besides," she added softly, "I'll help you with it," meaning the reading of it.

Which he knew very well because he coughed, saying: "Well, if you would. But if you cannot, I dessay I can manage myself. That is, if we go back. 'Tis only you saying it at the moment, Miss Minnie."

Nothing more was said.

At least half of the stew was left in the bowl. Miss Minnie had carefully bought some tough old stewing steak.

Looking at the remains, she said, "It can't be helped. Living in a town, if that's what you intend, there's no point in expecting otherwise. It is handy with a butcher just around the corner. Although I often get paid by a few poor old people this way, you can't expect me to bring a rabbit or a bit of partridge on my bicycle every week."

"I don't," said Mr Farrants.

"Nor a nice woodpigeon neither."

"Nor that," he replied testily.

Although Mr Farrants by his manner had not exactly

encouraged her, Miss Minnie decided that the best thing to do was to see Mr Fitz-Maurice as soon as possible, since the more she thought about it and delayed it, the more nervous she felt. For now everyone thought Mr Fitz-Maurice would be elected and actually take his place in the House of Commons, no less.

She would have preferred to talk to his political rival, Mr Perkins. He was Chairman of the Gas Works Road Residents Association and he too lived in Gas Works Road, at No. 3. He was one of the people, and he had various things like pots of marmite, grate polish and so on, put down in an exercise book and paid for on Fridays at the corner shop. He had pastry-like chins due to lack of exercise and he did not smile.

Whereas Mr Fitz-Maurice both smiled and, now it seemed at last, "understood" people, the old and the poor in particular. Mr Fitz-Maurice warmed to his task. He was carried away with it. The same Fitz-Maurice who would have dismissed a servant for taking a slice of rook pie now clasped the hands of the poor. They felt he understood them. He saw the poor people's shoes and shook his head. "It will not do!" he had muttered to an old man, bent with arthritis, whose only pleasure in life was toast and marmalade.

His eyes lit up with joy when he saw young people, particularly if their parents were there to observe it. Boys with tadpoles in jars looked up. Young girls, riveted still by the palms of their mothers' hands, warmth radiating on their heads, swivelled eyes. Grandfathers holding fly swats stopped in the act as the sleepy little winter flies danced drunkenly on the glass panes. Muffin men, ringing their handbells, trays on their heads, stopped ringing and selling, straightened up, war medals catching the sun.

All of them stopped and listened to Mr Fitz-Maurice. He called on the rows of red-and-yellow brick houses with their gleaming door knockers and polished door steps, front windows often full of brass pots, ferns and watching cats.

One old lady had asked him: "Well, what can I do for you?"

"You can vote for me," he had smiled.

"Perhaps I will, perhaps I won't," she had said. "And I've got work to do." But she said to herself: "Perkins is not a patch on him. Perkins don't stand a chance."

But he did not call at Gas Works Road, knowing the Farrants

His eyes lit up with joy when he saw young people.

to be there and thinking that a meeting would be embarrassing.

Mr Fitz-Maurice had not known before that he was a good speaker, that a certain kind of person was immediately impressed with him. The more aware he became of his success the more careless he became in his manner: the more enticing, the more charming. Here was a man, a gentleman, a landowner, someone who had been to places like Sebastopol, who had eaten rook pie, and yet who could talk to ordinary people as if they too were important. He had never known he could do it. He became infected with his own sense of well-being and caring. Even at home, at the long table, he asked after the butler's mother, only to be told that she had died three years previously.

So Miss Minnie was received by Mr Fitz-Maurice in that caring spirit when she arrived at his door.

"Excuse me, sir," the butler said, "Miss Minnie Maynard is outside. Shall I tell her to go?"

"No, Waters, no! Gordon pass the cheese, there's a good lad. Ask her to wait in the hallway, Waters, and offer her a glass of wine. Tell her I'll be there in a minute."

"Is he a relation of yours or something?" Mr Fitz-Maurice duly asked her when he had heard her business.

Miss Minnie looked him in the eye. "No, I just call regular and clean and help as best I can, which is what the vicar suggested in the first place. And it's him, the vicar, who 'as said you want Mr Farrants back."

"What if I do?"

"Then I'm saying, sir, there should be an agreement and, seeing that Mr Farrants hasn't had his reading glasses for years, he says I can do the arranging for him."

"What do you mean?" Mr Fitz-Maurice had started to redden.

"I mean, sir, about wages and the like. Then he can pay you rent for the 'ut and he'll be protected."

"Against what, may I ask?"

"Being turned out. And also there's water. If he's paying rent then he'll expect water to be piped through to his 'ut, and in a tap like most people has it."

"I don't think you realise . . . "

"Oh I do! I know you're a kind man who depends on people to vote. I've been to one of your meetings," she said softly, "you're ever so kind. All over, people talk about the new Member of Parliament caring for people."

"I'm not elected yet. There's Perkins. Look," he went on, "you come in here, you drink my wine . . . "

"It was offered."

" . . . and talk to me about water being laid on and so on. Do you realise that takin' back Farrants . . . "

"He's the best fencer and ditcher you ever had."

"Oh I agree. That's what's so upsettin'. But if you'll not interrupt. D'you realise I would be taking back a family of thieves?"

"If he'd been paid a wage like he was before you took him out of the General's cottage, as it is now, then his children wouldn't have done it."

"Stealin' is stealin'."

"I know it is, and I don't hold with it. But," she added, "you're not taking back thieves, not until the court sits and the magistrate says so. Not until then are they guilty."

"I will let Farrants know. I will think about it. No. 97 you say? Very well." Of course he knew what he would have to do. Miss Maynard, for all her impertinence, was right. Yes, he would give Farrants his water, pay him wages, take his rent, although it was most annoying. If, that is, he was going to be elected, due to his being a likeable and kind person.

Then he went to Gordon and the boy quivered as he listened.

"Your friends the Farrants children will be coming back. Georgina and Ferdinand, I believe."

"They are not my friends, Uncle."

"I am arrangin' for them to have water. These are humble people, good people, the salt of the earth. As their Member of Parliament, since I don't think Perkins will get in by a long shot, I must look after their needs."

"Yes, Uncle."

"Gordon, I want you to start tomorrow mornin'. You've a day left before you go back to school. Take a brush and some Vim. Get water from Mrs Portwine's up the road. Ghastly business goin' into the woods for it. Scrub it!"

"Uncle?"

"Before paintin' it needs to be cleaned. I'll get someone in the village to paint it all up nice, and you can do the preparin'."

*   *   *

But Mr Fitz-Maurice still forbade Mrs Portwine to collect herbs, which she said she could just have managed to do, weak as she was.

The way Mr Fitz-Maurice looked at it was that if there had been no trouble at the Portwine's he would not have spent "enormous sums of money paintin' the shed and gettin' the water in" in order to persuade Mr Farrants to return.

Uncomfortably aware of this hostility, Mr Portwine felt wretched and irritable. But it was not, he knew, a good idea to argue with Mrs Portwine in order to relieve his feelings.

So it was almost with pleasure that he said to Samantha: "A few days ago you were seen coming out of Mr Gould's bookshop."

"I was?"

"You were, you certainly were. What books did you buy?"

"They are hard to describe."

"Put in the effort then. *Oliver Twist*?"

"Something like that."

"Let me see them," he said.

"They were too heavy-going. I took them back."

"Where did you get the money from?" Mr Portwine tried again.

"From the extra pocket-money I get on account of the washing-up I do."

After a pause Mr Portwine snapped: "You are very trying, Samantha!"

Mrs Portwine sat in bed, listening, with her head to one side. "Samantha! What are you doing out there?"

"Dad's been telling me off that's all." She looked in.

"Why, child?"

"'Cause I was being annoying."

"I can understand that. But you have your good points, we've always said it."

"I was buying literature with my pocket-money."

"There we are!" said Mrs Portwine. "As I said, you're so good at times, annoyin' at others."

"Thank you, Mum."

"Doing all that washing-up. Not everybody", said Mrs Portwine, clenching her hands tightly under the bedclothes, "has a daughter like you."

Now this was more than Samantha could believe. Uneasily she stepped back. "Is there anything else?"

"No Samantha." Mrs Portwine was unflinching, like a snake coming out of a bed of bracken to look at the afternoon.

Downstairs, a customer was telling Mr Portwine about the bookshop.

"I've an old aunt who goes in there regular. She says, 'If you want to git me something for me birthday,' – with it often as not being ten months ahead – she says, 'then you git me a nice romance from Mr Gould's.'"

"I had my suspicions," said Mr Portwine.

"There's no harm in it."

"She's a deceitful girl," said Mr Portwine, more to himself.

Later, to his relief, Samantha caught the bus to town. Mrs Portwine was asleep after drinking a jug of beef tea, having assured Mr Portwine that she was recovering by degrees.

He searched in Samantha's bed and under it and in the drawers and wardrobes. He pulled up the rugs feeling for loose floor-boards. And there they were. He expected two or three books. There were so many they filled two boxes, each about twice the size of Miss Minnie's bicycle basket. He took them out into the shed and covered them with old potato sacks. "Fancy a daughter of mine reading nonsense like that. Romance!"

He did not think for a moment how one day he had dropped by mistake, no, almost flung, a plate of cucumber sandwiches at a young lady with pitch-black hair and twinkling eyes, and how that incident had ended in marriage.

When Samantha returned she straight away started the washing-up. She groaned, rubbing her balled fist over her face, damp with kitchen steam and with her sweat. Only one more plate! Suddenly she felt dreadfully weak. She made a cup of cocoa. Mr Portwine was polishing the tables for the morning's breakfasts, but she could not be bothered to say goodnight as she went up to her room.

Mr Portwine walked to the bottom of the stairs and started to polish the knob on the bannister. He had not replaced the floorboards. Then he heard a series of wails. He went up, determined to face Samantha about her lying, her deceitfulness and her choice of reading matter.

The following day Samantha did not get up, saying she was unwell.

Mr Portwine opened Samantha's door and said, not too unkindly: "Tomorrow, Samantha, it's up you get!"

But she did not.

The chaos was so bad that at one point, during a particularly busy breakfast, two unruly drivers were banging their plates on the table, the same men Mrs Portwine had to talk to like children before all the dreadful business with the Farrants.

Mr Portwine started to shake. Also he was running out of the sausage meat to which Mrs Portwine had added her special and secret herbs and a little of the darker and gamey meat. And now they were out there, his customers, as near to rioting as you please!

Mrs Portwine could hear it from upstairs. She banged on the floor, wanting to know what the commotion had been about. "None of it would have happened, Henry! None of it. To think of such behaviour in my café. All of it is your fault! The state we are in. Samantha is in bed. I'm in bed."

"I know very well."

"And do you care? If only you hadn't interfered," Mrs Portwine wailed. "The Farrants were doing the washing-up so nicely too!"

It was as if a door had been shut on all sound. On the one side, armies of men, tinklings and shouts, swords being beaten into shape, laden carts, baskets of food, children playing games in the dirt. Then a door shutting. Oak. A portcullis. And absolute silence. Not a sniff escaped from Mrs Portwine. Not a sigh as she realised what she had said.

At last she began to tell Mr Portwine the truth. "Oh Henry, can you ever forgive me? I saw the children steal, a long time ago. The very first time I'd forgotten to bolt the back door. I got up in the middle of the night to see to it, and saw them then."

"So then you always left it unbolted? Because you knew they did the washing-up?"

"Yes Henry. Yes."

"You must hate washing up. Really hate it, to have exploited children."

"They got their sausages. I got the washing-up done. I even took them for trap-rides."

"You exploited them!" His voice rose. "That amount of washing-up deserves ten times the value of what they took."

He paced up and down, stopping occasionally to talk excitedly. She simply folded her hands on top of the bed-clothes and pretended to be asleep. It was ridiculous. An insult!

"How could you believe I imagine you to be asleep! Am I a fool?" Mr Portwine shouted.

She only flapped her cheeks in the manner of being in deep sleep and even for a moment chattered her teeth together.

Then the knocker sounded and Mr Portwine left the room.

"Do come in, Sergeant," he said.

"Nice little place you have here, sir."

"What can I do for you?"

"It's just a small matter." He thought: there is something wrong with Mr Portwine. A disagreement? Money problems? "Everything alright, sir?" he said. Then he added deliberately: "I have called about evidence."

"What evidence?" asked Mr Portwine. "What do you mean?"

"Well, the Farrants business."

"Oh yes. Sergeant . . . " His hands went to his head. "I think perhaps we should not proceed."

"That won't be sensible, sir. Now do I take it you won't be willing to give evidence if it is brought to a trial?"

"If it comes to that, well, I suppose I must. But I do not really think . . . "

"Now sir, it's about the evidence. I can see you've got something on your mind, but if you would be so kind. You see," said the Sergeant, lowering his voice, "the evidence I took has in a manner of speaking 'gone off'."

"You mean the sausages?"

"Exactly! Now if I present these sausages in court as evidence the judge could rightly object, seeing that the court isn't really the place for smells and all that."

"So what do you want me to do about it?" asked Mr Portwine, being as patient as he could and still trembling because of the scene with Mrs Portwine.

"Replace them, sir, with a couple of pounds of fresh, so they'll be fit to take to court, should it come to it."

"Of course. I understand."

As the sergeant was leaving, he turned to Mr Portwine and said, "There's a small thing, keeps on coming back sir." He tapped his helmet. "In your statement – the odd things you noticed – owls screeching and so on. Not important. But there's one thing I can't understand. The bit about the plates being warm."

"Nor can't I," said Mr Portwine, quickly opening the door, and lapsing into the manner of speech that Mr Farrants and some of the carters used.

Then he made a few sausages but could not enter into the spirit of it. He looked at the piles of dirty plates.

If the Farrants children had done the washing-up, then Samantha could not have done it, at least not on those particular evenings! Oh of course, with the Farrants living in town, Samantha had been doing it recently. Bits of sausage in the rinsing water, streaks on the plates and dirty draining boards! For a long time, Mr Portwine reflected. He drank a pot of tea. He inspected the piles of dirty plates, hands behind his back.

When he was looking for the romances and pulling back the rugs he had noticed a hole in the floor where a pine knot had worked loose, or more likely been taken out by Samantha. So, he thought, she must have seen them too. Yes, I think that's what it's all about. I'm sure of it. He started humming. He took several teacloths off the line by the boiler and folded them neatly. Every now and then he muttered: "It all makes sense. I'm sure it does."

First of all he went to see Samantha. He put some of the nicely folded cloths on the foot of her bed.

"What is it, Dad?" she asked weakly.

"Teacloths," said Mr Portwine. "When I found these books, Samantha, I also found a letter. Couldn't make head nor tail of it. First of all it was written in your writing, then disguised. Left-handed."

Samantha turned her head slowly on the pillow.

"A practice letter, that's what it was," he continued, "and it was blackmail, wasn't it? Your cousin Felicity indeed!"

"I was playing about." Her voice was pitched high, anxious.

"You decided to take credit for it all. The Farrants children washing-up. Yes, I know about it all." He moved the carpet, pointing at the hole. "Just so you could ask for more pocket-money."

She said nothing.

"For more romances, wasn't it? D'you know what they do to people who blackmail?"

Samantha said weakly: "Dad, it's not as bad as all that."

"Oh yes it is, so you can get up straight away and start the washing-up. Straight away. Did you hear? Strange, I never heard about you buying the books, until recently, that is."

"The Farrants children did most of it for me, that's what I was blackmailing them for."

Then he went to see Mrs Portwine.

"Is that Samantha I can hear in the kitchen?"

"It is, my love."

"Oh Henry, I have been wrong. I will not deny it anymore. Yes, I have exploited the Farrants children." She paused, listening. "Is Samantha doing the washing-up?"

"She is. Yes, she is." He put the rest of the tea towels on her bed and patted them. Then asked her: "Why did you give Samantha extra pocket-money, knowing full well that she had not done the extra washing-up?"

"I could not let on, Henry, could I? And it was still worth it."

"Because you hate washing-up so much!"

"You understand. I was sure you would." She sat up in bed, smiling at him. "Right from when I was a young lady I did not like washing-up. You do remember, don't you, Henry? I mean, all those years ago. Such a ridiculous way to meet someone, having a lot of cucumber sandwiches thrown at you, but so romantic!"

Mr Portwine pointed to the teacloths. "I've got to clean the sausage machine."

"I've always hated it, Henry," she said uneasily.

But all Mr Portwine could say was: "The sooner you start the quicker it will be done."

7

All Is Not Lost

It was elegant in the Farrants' old cottage. The General would on no account have left his shoes to dry by the stove (having stuffed them with newspaper beforehand) as Mr Farrants had often done. Or leave opened jars of marmalade about, or allowed torn stuffing to have shown on the tea cosy.

In fact it was now so much to his liking and so comfortable that often he fell asleep in the afternoon, his mind crowded with memories of the East: of camel rides, trumpetings of elephants, military parades and so forth.

One afternoon, like this, he was reading a book. Now and then he waved it up and down as he struggled to keep awake. Then as it tumbled into his lap, the page number lost again, he would say: "Oh! Ah, yes!"

It was at one of these moments that Susan said, "Father, the people who lived in the hut – the people who had lived here once – the Farrants."

"Ah! Oh yes. What?" It was almost pleasant being interrupted like this, startled from half-sleep. He opened his book to read and almost as soon it fell to his lap. Deliciously, like this, he started to fitfully remember again. No one could imagine the sights and sounds of India! Lines of cavalry, no talking, heads up, sun flashing on the colours and metal. How could you tell a feller like Fitz-Maurice? Said he'd been to Sebastopol. If he had, that was all very well. But it did not make him a man of the world.

"The Farrants children, Father."

"Oh yes! Ah!"

"They will be appearing at Juvenile Court charged with stealing sausages from Mrs Portwine."

"Really? Oh well, I must say." He opened his book.

"Sometimes they would cook them over a fire in the woods.

Several times . . . "

"Yes of course."

"They were stolen sausages, Father. I also ate them in the woods and I knew they had been stolen."

"Would you mind repeating that? Did you say stolen sausages?"

"Yes Father."

"And you ate 'em, knowing them to have been stolen?"

"Yes Father."

"And you did this with, actually with those people from the hut?" The General's mind cleared. The tigers went back to the jungle, the reds and shell pinks slipped away from the vast evening clouds. The hyaenas stopped howling by the garbage bins outside the cookhouse. He was wide awake.

The sausage cooking was as good a thing I've ever done, Susan thought.

Half of her life had been spent in travelling, in moving, because of her father being a general. She knew from the look on his face now that another move would be planned. Only this time it would be because of what she had admitted to doing. And she only told him because she hoped he might be able to stop the case going to court.

She was right about her father. He spoke to the police, but only in a way to protect their own good name.

"Ah, Inspector. How d'you do. Case coming up soon, I believe?"

"In a few weeks, sir. It will be the Juvenile Court, of course, with a magistrate."

"You see, Inspector, my child's been seeing the hut children. Did they happen to mention it in their statements? The Farrants children."

"Mention what, sir?"

"Oh, their friendship and that sort of thing."

"In what way?"

"The fact is, she's been eating the things. In the woods."

"No mention of it here, sir," said the Inspector. "In any case if that part of it should come out, I'm quite sure your daughter did not know."

"Exactly so! Thought I'd mention it. Leaving the district. Wanted to get it sorted out first."

Then he spent some of the afternoon with Lady Eunice, finally calling to see Mr Fitz-Maurice.

"How's her Ladyship?"

"Very well," the General replied, having just left his wife thick lidded after an hour of weeping, listless on her sofa, the sun dazzling on the cottage walls, her finger prodding a marshmallow, her spirit gone. "I've decided to take a position abroad, so we'll be moving, Fitz-Maurice. Spent me life moving. Wife doesn't like the idea I must admit."

Mr Fitz-Maurice offered him a glass of port. He could feel the blood thumping at the back of his neck. "Is it somethin' wrong, I mean, amiss? Is perhaps the cottage damp?"

"No, no, no! My dear fellow! It's a beautiful cottage. Splendid view." Dash it, he thought, I like moving. Can't help it. Then there was Susan being such close friends with the Farrants. Good time to be moving. "To tell you the truth," the General said, "I'm not too happy about the business at the Portwines."

"I don't quite see . . ."

"The sausages. Not happy about the sausages."

"In what sense?"

The General, who now suddenly had no intention of giving details of his family's problems to Fitz-Maurice, Member of Parliament or not, replied: "It's simply . . . I don't like 'em!"

Mr Fitz-Maurice looked deeply puzzled.

The General added, by way of closing the conversation, prodding a finger at him, "You never know what's in 'em!"

*   *   *

Lately some of Mrs Portwine's customers had been saying things about the sausages.

But not so Mr Bert Whiting, who like Mr Farrants was employed by the council to cut the grass by the roadside. He said, "The sassages be as good as ever."

But a particularly rude carter, waving his fork, in spite of Mrs Portwine's presence, said, "Bert, 'e don't taste nothing."

"I'll tell you what, Mrs Portwine," said another "they're alright, but that's all. They'm the same as any other sassages!"

"Like the ones you can git anywhere," said the one who had

been waving his fork.

Mrs Portwine later confided: "Henry, without Mr Fitz-Maurice's permission to go on his land I cannot get all the herbs and seasonings for the sausage-meat."

"He will change his mind."

"We are faced with ruin in the meantime."

So first thing next morning, aided by a heavy mist, Mrs Portwine had gone off across the fields. She carried her large herb-gathering bag. Sometimes she rubbed the leaves to get the smell off them, making sure of what she had gathered. Listening carefully she then set about finding what she called "some seasonings".

Although she would normally let the birds improve in a locked outdoors shed, from which Mr Portwine was banished, under the circumstances she had the seasonings cooked and minced by midday. Mr Portwine had the sausage-meat made by late lunchtime. The verge-cutter was there.

"Try one out on Bert," said Mr Portwine.

"A waste of time," she replied.

Then the rude carter came in. "I'm giving it one more try, missis," he said.

"Free on the house." Mrs Portwine smiled.

He tasted it, winked several times, wiped his mouth, then asked for the mild-flavoured mustard and a slice of bread.

"Now for Mr Fitz-Maurice!" she muttered.

He was sitting on his verandah, enjoying a glass of wine in the afternoon sun, when he saw Mrs Portwine coming up the drive with her basket. "What on earth?" he said to himself. It was the butler's day off. "Gordon!" he called, but there was no reply. He called out to her through the window: "Over here. I'm on the verandah."

"Oh, Mr Fitz-Maurice."

"Yes, well, what is it?"

Mrs Portwine put her basket on a chair. Its contents were covered with a white cloth. "I've come to say how sorry my husband is to have persecuted those poor children, and to have annoyed you by doing so."

He inclined his head.

"I read the local paper," she said, "all about Mr Farrants."

There had been an article about Mr Fitz-Maurice's nephew

cleaning the hut and about it being repainted at great cost. There was a picture of Mr Farrants standing outside No. 97 Gas Works Road, in his baggy trousers which were too short, holding his cap, his moustache drooping. Such a common-looking fellow really, Mr Fitz-Maurice had thought. But what splendid publicity!

"The help you give to those who have suffered misfortune is well known," Mrs Portwine continued.

And is gainin' me some more votes, he thought.

"We are suffering," she said. "Oh I know it was because of my husband's cruelty: little children, to think of it! But will you not help *me*? If I am not allowed to walk about on your lovely estate looking for herbs and seasonings," here she paused and lifted the edge of the cloth which covered her basket, "we will be ruined."

"Well I . . . " he said.

Then she took the sausages out and held them to him. He looked at them fascinated. "I dislike to see anyone sufferin'," he said in a quiet way, "so you'd better carry on with the herb gatherin' and all that."

As he took them she said, "Twenty minutes, medium, they'll be done nicely. Put a fork in, let the meat pop out and brown a little." Then she left him.

Mrs Portwine smiled to herself. She took a short cut across the edge of his barley field, stooping to pick a herb, then rubbing it between her thumb and middle finger. She noticed a column of smoke rising up over the tops of the trees, in the direction of the Farrants. It was four o'clock in the afternoon. She shivered. A mist was forming again. At first she thought, that will be Mr Farrants with his creosote fire, although there seemed to be more smoke than usual. She mused: "They'll be nicely settled in again by now!"

But gradually the flames began to light up the underside of the rising mist. The vicar too had seen the fire on his way to welcome the Farrants family back to the parish. By now, both he and Mrs Portwine were running towards the shed.

With great presence of mind Mr Farrants had attached the garden hose, which was a moving-in present from Miss Maynard, to the new water supply. But by the time the brigade had arrived it was all over. It was too hot to get to the tap to turn it off, and Mr Farrants stood there with the hose in his hand.

The reporter from *The News* arrived. "You again, Mr Farrants! You two children! Stand there, that's right. Keep hold of the hose, Mr Farrants, head up. There we are."

Georgie held her wrist to her mouth, biting the skin, her eyes red, her other arm round Ferdie.

The sack of parsnips had been put outside the back door, for Mr Farrants had not wanted them in the house. They were the only things saved, apart from one or two personal items which Georgie had managed to put in her pocket before being dragged out by her father.

*   *   *

The local evening paper managed to print the story of Mr Farrants' tragedy and the election of Mr Fitz-Maurice in the same issue. At the victory party in the Manor, the vicar repeatedly tried to speak to Mr Fitz-Maurice privately, but was told again: "Not now, Vicar. Whatever it is, it can wait. I'm celebratin'!"

So the vicar went to Mr Fitz-Maurice's stables where the Farrants' family were being housed for the night. He said to them: "All is not lost!"

To which Mr Farrants replied: "Well, with respect, Vicar, seeing as we're sitting on the straw and soon we'll be able to see the stars through the gap in the roof, and seeing I'm wearing an old pin-striped suit given me because what I was wearing at the time I've throwed away on account of them being torn and burned . . . "

"Oh Dad!" interrupted Ferdie, "we did at least 'ave supper in the Manor kitchen."

The vicar was now pacing up and down and becoming quite agitated. "Mark my words, Mr Farrants, all is not lost!"

"You'm not referring to the parsnips Vicar?" asked Mr Farrants, his eyes getting smaller.

"Indeed I'm not, I do assure you. But now I must get back to the party!" And so he left them.

"Vicar, have some champagne!"

"I must have a word with you."

"I'm sure it can wait," snapped Mr Fitz-Maurice.

"Where's the General? I can't see the General," said Mrs Fellowes from Barton Hall, "and dear Lady Eunice, of course. I hear she has not been well."

"As far as I know . . . " the vicar began.

"They are not here," said Mr Fitz-Maurice.

"Now, Fitz-Maurice," the vicar said as soon as Mrs Fellowes had scampered off to another guest, "I insist. I wish to talk to you privately."

"Very well. Although I must say, your insistence is unwelcome, Vicar."

"There is no law against turning people out of a cottage if they live in it rent-free because they are employed by the owner."

"Well?"

"But there should be! You should never have turned out the Farrants from their cottage because Mrs Farrants died."

"Vicar, this is an outrage!"

"It is, it is!"

"She did housework for me. When the poor woman died . . . "

"You painted it up and let it to the General."

"Vicar, your bishop will hear of this. Now sir, I intend to return to the party, which, by the way, you can leave instantly!"

"But Mr Fitz-Maurice, I have to tell you that the fire at Mr Farrants' hut was started deliberately."

"Oh? If it was, then they must suffer. The Farrants, I suppose? Liked Gas Works Road after all, is that it?"

"No, it was your nephew. It was Gordon."

"How dare you say so!" Mr Fitz-Maurice had gone very pale and had almost whispered the words.

"I saw it. I was about to call to welcome them back and I saw Gordon running backwards and forwards several times from the creosoting tank to the hut. I could not make out what he was doing. It was difficult because of the mist. Then there was a glow at his feet and he ran off."

"This is an insult! How could you possibly say it was Gordon? And did he see you?"

"He would not have done so. And another person saw him moments later. Stumbling, running through the strip of trees by the barley field, on his way back to the Manor."

Mr Fitz-Maurice's fingers, his shoulders, were shaking with rage. "I cannot accept it!"

"She has already told me she will swear a statement, if need be, in front of a solicitor."

"And who is this lady, may I ask?"

"Mrs Portwine."

Some time later Mr Fitz-Maurice and the vicar rejoined the party.

"You do not look well," said one of the Misses Garnets from the Gate House, "poor Mr Fitz-Maurice, you have worked so hard. It's a lovely party, don't you think so, Vicar?"

"I do, I do indeed." He smiled broadly.

"Did you say Lady Eunice was not well?" she asked.

"I did not," said Mr Fitz-Maurice.

"Is that why they are not here – the General and Lady Eunice?"

"They have gone, madam! That is why they are not here. Left!"

"Oh, I did not know. How sudden. Was something wrong?"

"Have you a new tenant in mind for the cottage?" asked another lady. "I have a niece, just married to the Hon. Freddie Gore – perhaps until they find a place of their own . . . "

"It is spoken for," said Mr Fitz-Maurice.

"For whom? How interesting!"

"Farrants. Now if you will excuse me! Ladies!"

By the time Mr Farrants had been told to go to the Manor for breakfast next day it was nearly twelve o'clock. He thanked the butler again for his gift of the pin-striped suit, then they sat down and enjoyed a breakfast of kippers, followed by toast and marmalade, ignorant of the sudden change in their fortunes.

"Dad," said Georgie, "now that we've lost everything, will you and Miss Minnie still be marryin'?"

Mr Farrants put his knife down sharply. "When did you find that out?"

"Well it was plain enough to see, Dad."

"It was," said Ferdie.

After a pause Mr Farrants said, "There never will be no one

". . . except as he's a gentleman in a pin-striped suit."

to take the place of your mother. Nor Miss Minnie, come to that. But we ain't marrying yet, as you say my dears, with all this going on!" He rose from the table. "Now I'd best see Mr Fitz-Maurice for today's orders, for I'm employed by him, and perhaps he can suggest some better sleeping arrangements for tonight."

The butler was not in the kitchen. So Mr Farrants went into the hallway where he saw a young housemaid.

"Would you please ask Mr Fitz-Maurice what he wants me to do?"

"The name sir?"

"It's Farrants," he said, smiling at being spoken to in this way.

But the girl who had just started work at the Manor and was easily flustered could not remember the name. She simply told Mr Fitz-Maurice that a gentleman wished to see him.

"Come now, what sort of gentleman?"

"Well, I don't rightly know sir, except as he's a gentleman in a pin-striped suit."

"Oh well, best send him in then. And bring me the sherry and two of me best glasses in case I'm in for a bit of entertainin'."

8

The Verdict

Mr Ernest Popjoy was wearing a black gown, because of his position as Court Usher. He bent down to Georgie and Ferdie and whispered loudly: "You're not nervous, I hope?"

Mr Farrants sat with Miss Minnie on the bench behind the children. He looked straight ahead.

"You are not frightened of all this?" Mr Popjoy waved proudly towards the raised platform where in a moment the three magistrates would assemble. "When I call you," he said, "you will go into the witness box. Do you see it?" He glanced at Mr Farrants and blew through his teeth, making a very quiet and steamy sort of whistle which could barely be heard.

It was because of his generally odd habits and his shabbiness (although Mrs Popjoy did her best to conceal it with constant stitching and pressing) that he had been Court Usher for many years. He was likely to remain so, as his wife said, until "Kingdom come". He played cards every Sunday afternoon with his wife, sometimes with neighbours as well, who, living in a poor district, looked up to him with his court connections.

"The court will stand!" called out Mr Popjoy.

So everyone in court stood up, Georgie and Ferdie with a light-headed feeling. Mr Farrants seemed shorter than ever.

Major Benson looked the court over, then gazed particularly at Mr Farrants and the children. he even looked at Mr Popjoy, who shifted uncomfortably. The Major had a large face. His mouth open and shut like the poor goldfish at fairs. He had white moustaches.

The two other members of the bench were ladies. One of them was styled as a housewife, also she happened to be Lord Gladwyn's niece. She looked as if she had left her gas oven on high instead of medium but was determined not to be put out by it.

The other was the widow of Colonel Sanders, late Town Clerk. She looked very kind. She gazed serenely at the court below with a soft half-smile, as if her heart was full of the knowledge of the sorrows of those before her.

Bending down, Mr Popjoy whispered to Mr Farrants: "They take it in turns. Today it's the Major. You may be thankful for that. He is the most lenient. The kind-looking lady would send them down to prison if she had half a chance." To the children he said, "When you enter the witness box, do not be frightened of him, and speak clearly. Do not mumble."

Ferdie was first in the witness box.

"Is your name Ferdinand Farrants?" The Major leaned forward, mouth opening and shutting, in a kindly way saying again: "Come, boy, answer the question. Very well, then, the other defendant may enter the box since he is tongue-tied. We will try again with him later . . . . Are you Georgina Farrants?"

She nodded.

"Yes or no?"

"Yes."

"Address me as Your Honour."

"Yes please, Your Honour."

"Now Georgina, you have promised to tell the truth. But first of all the Inspector will read your statements to the court."

After the Inspector sat down, Major Benson coughed importantly, then said, "Where is the exhibit?"

Mr Popjoy handed a packet up to the magistrates, saying: "Your Honour."

"So these are the sausages. Made by Mrs Portwine, you say. Very well." He looked severely at Georgina in the witness box.

"There are never two pounds of sausages there," whispered Lord Gladwyn's niece, who was acknowledged by her friends and neighbours to be a dab hand at cooking. "There's three of them missing. I always do toad-in-the-hole on Tuesdays and I should know."

"In that case," said the Major, "we will call the officer who was in charge of the case. Usher!"

"Now, Sergeant," the Major continued, when Bunny Wheeler took the stand. "The statement says 'I took 2 lbs of sausages on that occasion'. Here we have only 1½ lbs. I can state that with authority."

Lord Gladwyn's niece nodded several times.

"What happened to the missing sausages? We have to be particular in these matters."

Unprepared, surprised at being called when the defendant had pleaded guilty, and uncomfortable in the extreme, the Sergeant answered gruffly: "I ate 'em." Hastily correcting himself, he added: "I ate them, Your Honour, but saw no harm, Your Honour, since they are not the sausages that was stolen, with respect."

There was a little stir in the court. The Police Inspector looked steadily at the ceiling, Mr Popjoy adjusted his gown and Lord Gladwyn's niece coughed.

Major Benson asked quietly: "When was the offence committed?"

The Inspector rose. "Fourteen weeks ago, Your Honour."

The Major conferred with the kind-looking magistrate, then bent his head to one side to Lord Gladwyn's niece. After a pause he looked up. "Please tell the court in your own words, Sergeant, why we do not have the original sausages in court."

The Sergeant spoke the truth because he was a truthful man, and also because nothing else fitted. "I ate them, Your Honour."

The Inspector broke his pencil in half, holding the remains of it in his clenched fist. A deep silence filled the court.

"Do I understand, Sergeant, that you have eaten the evidence?"

"I replaced it, sir, in respect to the court, seeing that high-smelling sausages might offend."

Mr Popjoy smiled, but caught the eye of the kind-looking lady magistrate and wished that he had not.

"But these sausages, in front of the court, are fresh," said the Major. "How can these be the replacements referred to?"

"They are not, Your Honour," the Sergeant said in a near whisper.

"How many lots of 'evidence' have you had from the, what

"Here we have only 1½ lbs. I can state that with authority."

is it, the Portwine's?"

"Eleven all told, Your Honour."

"And even the last lot – which you have finally allowed the court to behold – have been ravaged. Have you anything to say to explain your conduct?"

"Yes, Your Honour."

"I am glad, Sergeant. Inspector, are you noting this line of questioning?"

"Very much so, Your Honour," said the Inspector, rising to his feet.

"And will be considering what action to take?"

"Very much so, sir."

Major Benson conferred with the other magistrates. "What then, Sergeant, explains it?" he asked.

"Well, Your Honour, I was visiting Mr Portwine regularly, pursuing a particular line of enquiry. As a result of this questioning Your Honour, Mr Portwine has handed me a letter not five minutes ago outside the court."

The letter was passed up to the Major, and after a quiet exchange of words with the other magistrates which no one else could hear, and a great deal of gaping by Major Benson, it was announced that the court would adjourn for ten minutes to consider the contents of the letter.

When, after the interval, Sergeant Walker re-entered the box, he said, "I could not understand, Your Honour, why the dishes were warm. Mr Portwine got excited every time I mentioned it and usually gave me an extra pound of sausages, which I could have taken to mean, Your Honour, that because of his anxiety about the warm dishes and my line of questioning, that the course of justice . . . "

"Sergeant, I will have plenty to say to you about the course of justice and about your own conduct. Please allow the court to decide on Mr Portwine's."

"Your Honour."

"You may stand down, Segeant."

Mr Portwine was only thankful that because it was a private hearing in a Juvenile Court – all the people present being relatives and the like – and because the children had pleaded guilty, there had been no reason for Mrs Portwine to attend.

Expanding on his letter, prodded relentlessly by the Major,

smiled at by the kind lady magistrate, looked at by Lord Gladwyn's niece, he told the bench about Mrs Portwine and her dislike of washing-up, and about Samantha and her romances and the lengths to which that wicked girl had gone. At the end of it all he was in a pitiable state.

Without consulting his fellow magistrates Major Benson said fiercely: "You should stand up to Mrs Portwine, sir."

"Your Honour?"

"It is a pity, Mr Portwine, that Mrs Portwine is not here. She may well be where you are now, Mr Portwine, if the court decides a separate action should be taken. That is all."

"Step down," called Mr Popjoy.

"We have here an unusual case." Major Benson looked severely at Mr Farrants. "We have a father's greed. Yes, Mr Farrants, a passion, a lust for sausages. Then Sergeant Walker eats these sausages of Mrs Portwine's. You will note they have not been referred to as Mr Portwine's sausages, although I understand that gentleman spends many hours at his sausage machine. That is a reflection, ladies and gentlemen, on the personality of Mrs Portwine . . . As to the Sergeant, he calmly claims that in the pursuit of enquiries he has eaten more than eleven pounds of sausages! . . . Then I understand there is another child, who risked her family's good name. Do we know the name of this child?"

At this point Lord Gladwyn's niece whispered to him.

The Major coughed and said, "We do not of course know this child. But we know *these* children. Georgina and Ferdinand, who were willing to slave away in Mrs Portwine's kitchen in the middle of the night in order to take sausages . . . Then at the centre is a lady who has schemed, who has exploited children to avoid the washing-up. And a daughter whose passion for romances, and the need for secrecy in the purchase of these books, drove her to blackmail. She did not realise her mother knew of the Farrants children stealing. And her mother had to keep silent to make sure the washing-up was done. Now Ferdinand. Can you speak yet boy? The boy can speak? He has not an impediment of speech? He has not? Very well. Ferdinand and Georgina, do you understand that you have stolen sausages, that you set out to steal and that is wrong? The bench takes a very serious view of people who steal, whatever the reason. I do not want to see you in court again. Do you understand?"

"Yes, Your Honour," said Georgie.

"Your Honour," said Ferdie.

"Now, I have read the vicar's report and the school report. They are good, although there's a mention here about reading. If I were a parent of such children I would be proud to have these reports of them," he said, looking at Mr Farrants. "The plot to exploit these children – we have carefully worked it out, washing-up for just under 2d an hour – would not have been possible unless the children had a conscience. They have a conscience, Mr Farrants, and it is a credit to you. The plot to blackmail them would not have succeeded had not the children a sense of honour. They had promised Samantha not to let Mrs Portwine know ... Then our police! An officer of the law has repeatedly eaten the evidence! ... It is without hesitation that I dismiss the case!"

As the magistrates rose from their seats Mr Popjoy called: "The court will stand!"

Ferdie was holding Miss Minnie's hand. Georgie had her arms nearly around Mr Farrants, laughing then sobbing and quickly turning her face when she did so; Mr Farrants was patting her head, for all the world as if he was comfortably searching for eggs in the hen-box.

Outside the court the Major called the usher.

"Your Honour?"

Major Benson bowed to the other two magistrates and made his way to Mr Popjoy. "How are your children, Usher? Do they attend school?" Then, looking to the left and right, he said quietly: "The exhibit, Mr Popjoy. The exhibit! The sausages, man! What's left of them. Curiosity. Can't help feeling it."

"Your Honour?"

"Right first time. That's it!" said the Major. "My car is at the front of the building. Passenger seat. What a mild winter we are having so far!"

* * *

Mrs Portwine, to the satisfaction of everybody who had a

knowledge of "the trouble at Mrs Portwine's", as it later became known, provided most of the food for the wedding feast. Sausages played a prominent part in it, both hot and cold. Mr Portwine, who was suffering from depression, had an unfortunate run of small sausages, all of which were served on sticks.

Georgie did some of the cooking, making tarts with the special jam, the only trouble being that the wild strawberries had hardened, perhaps because of their age. There were enough only for members of the family and were served after everyone else had gone. Georgie had saved the pot from the fire. Now, she knew, was the time to eat it. She had a feeling of being certain that it was the right thing to do, and held long imaginary conversations as she was cooking them.

One of Mrs Portwine's friends made five dozen of her favourite chocolate éclairs, dusted lightly with icing sugar. The vicar's wife had contributed a boxful of cucumber sandwiches. The vicar ate some of these, then, bestowing affectionate glances on his wife, tried an éclair. But he avoided the sausages, in fact he turned from them. He had emptied his sermon drawer, cleaned it out, after the court hearing. He had in a sense put them behind him.

The church had been full. Apart from the village people, the carter who had moved them back to the hut was there, and some neighbours from 171, 252, 150 and 30 Gas Works Road. Also Mr and Mrs Perkins from No. 3.

Mr Fitz-Maurice was at the reception although no one could remember having invited him. He had nodded, unsmiling, at Mr Perkins, staring at him for rather longer than was polite.

"At least he's keeping himself to himself," said Minnie, referring to Mr Fitz-Maurice. "And Gordon is not here of course," she added.

"I can't say I'm sorry," said Georgie, who had heard he had been sent to Scotland shortly after the court case.

"Has it occurred to you my dear, that Gordon was jealous? I have always thought," Minnie coloured slightly, "that it was such a nice little family even in the shed and all . . . and Gordon with an uncle like that and no parents to speak of . . . "

"Oh I do see that," agreed Georgie.

"And then being asked to clean the shed must have been

Columbine has rampaged over the black remains of the hut.

the last straw, going to his 'ead in a manner of speaking."

Although of course not at the reception, Major Benson very kindly sent a small present: a silver mustard pot and spoon.

He became a regular visitor to Mrs Portwine's and said once: "Portwine! Portwine, I'm glad to see you're standing up to Mrs Portwine. I'm glad for your sake sir."

*   *   *

Now columbine has rampaged over the black remains of the hut, its white, horn-shaped flowers smelling a little sharp. Foxgloves have spread over the garden. A few cabbages not cut and put into sacks the previous year (how long ago it seems!) have grown tall, ready to seed. There is the smell of pollen and grasses everywhere. Gnats circle in clouds over the ditch and rabbits forage in the old garden without bothering to look up. The water in the ditch, grown over with weeds, is warm and smelling of the manure off the fields.

At the weekends Ferdie helps with the cutting of beansticks, having written permission from Mr Fitz-Maurice, and he cooks his cheese on an old shovel like the one Mr Farrants uses.

Georgie works at Mrs Portwine's for a proper wage, four (early) evenings a week. Like Ferdie, she can read now due to Minnie's help and a good position on the school benches. She has a better taste in books than Samantha ever had.

Only Georgie and Ferdie know about Mrs Portwine's "herb gathering and seasonings", and if they see her in the fields they simply make a point of looking the other way.